Alaina gazed at Rafa... figure, heart thudding.

Memories were clamoring to come back in, memories of her brief but unforgettable time with Rafaello on that magical, long-ago Caribbean island. For a moment she just stood there, faint with the aftershock of seeing Rafaello walk back into her life.

"Mummeee!"

She gave a gasp. Joey was emerging through the rotating door into the hotel and he hurtled toward the reception desk, little face alight with delight.

In horror, the world turned into slo-mo, paralyzing her. She could not move, not an inch. Joey reached the desk, placed his little hands on the edge, standing on tiptoes to see her, his smile beaming. But her eyes were not on him. They had gone, as if dragged by weights she could not counter, to the bank of elevators at the far end of the lobby.

She saw Rafaello pause in the act of pressing the button. Saw his hand drop away, saw him turn around. Saw his eyes go to Joey, hear him cry out *"Mummeee!"* again in excited greeting.

Saw Rafaello's expression change. His body freeze.

Julia James lives in England and adores the peaceful verdant countryside and the wild shores of Cornwall. She also loves the Mediterranean—so rich in myth and history, with its sunbaked landscapes and olive groves, ancient ruins and azure seas. "The perfect setting for romance!" she says. "Rivaled only by the lush tropical heat of the Caribbean—palms swaying by a silver-sand beach lapped by turquoise waters... What more could lovers want?"

Books by Julia James

Harlequin Presents

Billionaire's Mediterranean Proposal
Irresistible Bargain with the Greek
The Greek's Duty-Bound Royal Bride
The Greek's Penniless Cinderella
Cinderella in the Boss's Palazzo
Cinderella's Baby Confession
Destitute Until the Italian's Diamond
The Cost of Cinderella's Confession
Reclaimed by His Billion-Dollar Ring
Contracted as the Italian's Bride

Visit the Author Profile page
at Harlequin.com for more titles.

The Heir She Kept from the Billionaire

JULIA JAMES

HARLEQUIN
PRESENTS

HARLEQUIN®
PRESENTS™

Recycling programs for this product may not exist in your area.

ISBN-13: 978-1-335-59345-0

The Heir She Kept from the Billionaire

Harlequin Enterprises ULC
22 Adelaide St. West, 41st Floor
Toronto, Ontario M5H 4E3, Canada
www.Harlequin.com

Printed in Lithuania

MIX
Paper | Supporting responsible forestry
FSC® C021394

The Heir She Kept
from the Billionaire

For my editor, Emma Marnell—many thanks for all
your work on this, our first novel together.

PROLOGUE

ALAINA ASHCROFT WATCHED the hotel limo ease away from under the shaded portico, setting off down the long, hibiscus-lined drive towards the highway. She swallowed. Hard.

So he was going. Heading back to the airport, back to Italy, back to his own life—just as he had said he would. Demolishing all her hopes that he might extend his time here on the island, spend more time with her. That he might want to do so. Might want, perhaps, something more than holiday time with her...

Might want to take me back to Italy with him...

There was a tightness in her chest, as if something sharp was piercing her. Hadn't her mother warned her, from her own pitiful experience, how careful she must be lest she end up like her? Wanting what she could not have...yearning for it... For a man who did not want her... hoping all the time that he did...

As I have been hoping...

She swallowed again, turning away. Her hopes had been dashed. Now all she could do was get on with her own life. She had work to do, and work must be her therapy.

He's gone—and there's an end to it. Nothing more will

come of it, and my life will go on just as it did before. As if we'd never met. Never romanced at all…

But in that, as it turned out, she was completely mistaken…

CHAPTER ONE

Five years later...

RAFAELLO RANIERI STRETCHED out his long legs and crossed his ankles in a leisurely manner, relaxing back into the capacious first-class airline seat, then extracted a law journal from his briefcase to while away the flight to London.

As one of Italy's top lawyers, in great demand by a large number of the country's elite families for whom he and his law firm provided invaluable services when it came to tricky matters of tax efficiency, inheritance conflicts, troublesome offspring or annoyingly avaricious ex-spouses, he needed to keep abreast of his field—not just in respect of the Italian legal system, but wherever his wealthy clients might find themselves in need of his highly respected and extremely well-remunerated, expertise.

It was just such a client who necessitated this trip to London, to consult with his counterpart law firm based in the city's Inns of Court. He would be arriving too late to see them this evening, and as he was flying back to Rome the next day he had decided to overnight not in his customary hotel on Park Lane but in one of the nearby airport hotels. Tomorrow he would have a working lunch with his counterpart, then take a late-afternoon flight to Rome. A brief visit to the UK, but nothing untoward about it. Which was the way he liked to live his life. Calmly and smoothly.

His face shadowed a moment. 'Calmly and smoothly' had not been the way his mother had lived her unhappy life. His father, now living in semi-retirement from the highly prosperous family law firm, the management of which he had handed over to Rafaello, his son, had condemned her as neurotic and needy. His parents' disastrous marriage had only confirmed to Rafaello that his own chosen path—judiciously selected affairs with women who never wanted more than he was prepared to offer them, never wanted more than he wanted from their time together—was the wisest course for himself.

He felt his thoughts flicker. There had been one woman, once…

On a Caribbean island, with silver sand beaches, palms swaying in the tropical breeze…a perfect place for romance. And she had been perfect for a romance in such a place. Beautiful, passionate, ardent. He had desired her the moment he had seen her, and their affair had been all that he had wanted it to be.

Until she'd shown that she wanted more time with him than he had been prepared to offer her.

Then he'd driven away from her in the sleek hotel limo, towards the airport that would take him back to Italy, to the life that suited him very well—the life he was still leading now and intended to go on leading. Smooth and unruffled—just the way he liked it to be.

Alaina was harassed, but was not letting it show. That would be unprofessional. As one of the assistant managers at the hotel, she was well-schooled in presenting only an air of calm competence. So the fact that she was manning the reception desk because two of the staff had gone off sick and one was still a trainee must remain quite invisible to incoming and outgoing guests. So, too, the fact that she was running late to collect Joey.

She'd managed to put a call in to Ryan, with whom she'd 'paired' at the nursery, to bail each other out if work got in the way of the strict collection times enforced by the extremely good and therefore extremely popular nursery where Joey was enrolled. Thankfully he had agreed to collect Joey, along with his own four-year-old daughter, Betsy. He'd give both children tea at his house, then deliver Joey to her after he'd returned Betsy to her mother, who lived not very far away with her second husband. By that time the evening reception staff would be on, and Alaina could go off duty, clocking back in after she'd delivered Joey to nursery in the morning.

The system worked well—if sometimes stressfully, as today—allowing her to continue her job, which was both financially necessary and good from a career perspective. But being a full-time working mother of a small child brought its own pressures.

And unlike Ryan, who shared custody with his ex-wife, she was a full-time single parent.

But that was my choice.

Because otherwise she'd have had to disclose the existence of a child who'd never been planned or anticipated to a man who had no interest in her. However much she might have wished otherwise.

It was not to be—leave it at that...

The entrance of a flurry of guests delivered by the airport shuttle—one of the secondary London airports, situated out in the Home Counties, away from the capital, but always extremely busy for all that—demanded her attention.

She had just finished registering the guests when she heard the front doors open again. She glanced up, professional smile ready on her face. It wasn't time for the next shuttle, so it must be a self-drive or taxi arrival. But as she lifted her head the smile froze on her face.

To be replaced by an expression of complete and absolute disbelief.

Rafaello stopped dead. Unconsciously, his grip on his briefcase and the handle of his carry-on tightened. Then, as his eyes met those of the woman standing behind the reception desk, he said, *'Alaina?'*

He walked towards her, aware of conflicting emotions in his head. Shock was uppermost—that was to be expected. But there was something more, too, which right now he did not have time to analyse. He was dealing with the moment—that was all.

He schooled his expression as he approached. With his trained sense of observation he saw she had paled, and her face had tensed. Then, like him, she schooled her expression into neutrality.

'Rafaello—how extraordinary!'

Her voice was light, but he could tell she was deliberately making it so, that it was an effort for her. The tension in her face—and in her immediately veiled eyes—remained.

He allowed himself the very slightest of smiles. 'Well, these things do happen,' he answered, with a quizzical lift of one eyebrow.

'You're not on my reservation list,' she responded blankly.

He gave a shake of his head. 'No—I made the decision not to bother with going into London tonight on the flight. I take it you have availability?'

He saw her swallow, and it was clear to him that she was fighting for a veneer, at least, of normality. He could see a pulse beating at her throat, the faintest flush of colour staining her cheeks. It only enhanced her beauty...

He pulled his thoughts back. It was five years since her striking beauty had beguiled him on his visit to the Caribbean island where one of his most lucrative and much-divorced clients lived and had required his presence to initiate yet another divorce. Client dealt with, he'd indulged in a holiday for himself—and indulged, too, in a very enjoyable romance to enhance his time there.

Alaina had been working not where he himself had been staying—one of the fabled Falcone hotels—but at a more modest four-star hotel next door. He had seen her sunning herself on the beach as he'd strolled along one afternoon and that had been all it had taken.

She had been as responsive to his interest in her as he had wanted.

Perhaps too much so...

For all her very beguiling charms, he had been aware that she would have been more than happy for their encounter to become more than a mere holiday romance. He had drawn back from closer involvement—as he always did. It was more prudent so to do.

Yet, prudent as it might have been, he'd been conscious of faint regret as he'd headed back to the airport at the end of his stay.

His eyes rested on her now. She had matured in the five years since their time together, and unlike on the laid-back island she looked brisk and businesslike, in a crisply styled suit with neat lapels, her hair drawn back into a tight French plait, and only minimal make-up on her face.

Despite his best intentions, he felt memory spear.

Her...lying in bed...her glorious mane of dark hair tumbled and tousled and her luminous eyes holding his... her lush mouth soft as velvet...

He tamped it down. Stamped it down. It was not appropriate for this completely by-chance, unsought encounter.

'Yes. Yes, of course.'

Her voice was staccato, and he knew why. Knew why her eyes had veiled, even though she was looking at him straight on. She broke her gaze to look at the computer screen, flicking it to another page. Then looked back at him.

'Would you prefer a garden view or a lake view?' she asked politely, the dutiful hotel receptionist.

'Which is quieter?'

'Both are quiet, but the lake view rooms are closer to the car park.'

'Garden view,' he answered. 'Only one night,' he added.

She gave a distracted nod, tapping the keyboard. Not bothering to ask his name, which she knew perfectly well, or his nationality.

She knew so much else that was personal as well...

Again, to his displeasure, he felt memory distract him. She knew every centimetre of his body...how he liked his coffee...what food he liked.

How he liked to make love...

As did he know her. In the time they'd spent together they had acquired a lot of information about each other.

Too much?

Oh, not just lifestyle details, or even their respective sexual preferences—not that he would dwell on that right now—but more than that.

Information about what each wanted from life.

And from each other.

He shut down the memory. Unnecessary, unwanted. Unwelcome.

'Will you be dining with us tonight?'

Alaina's politely professional enquiry was timely. He gave a nod, and she entered the information on the screen, then turned to reach for his room key.

For just a moment, Rafaello found himself on the point of saying, *Have dinner with me*.

Good sense silenced him. For a start it was unlikely she would be allowed to dine with a guest, and anyway…

Seeing Alaina again like this, out of the blue, was to no purpose. His time with her all those years ago had been good—OK, he allowed mentally, *memorably* good—but it was long over, and that was the way it should remain. He'd made his decision back then not to take things any further, and there was no reason to question that.

His veiled gaze rested on her as she handed him his key with a professional smile accompanied by her own equally veiled gaze. Was there the slightest tremble in her hand as she held the folder out to him?

'I hope you enjoy your stay with us,' she was saying to him now, in her smiling, impersonal, professional way.

He gave an answering, equally impersonal smile as he took the key, then took hold of his carry-on again, turning to walk towards the elevators at the far end of the lobby. He was conscious he should have said something—made some innocuous remark acknowledging that they knew each other, some passing pleasantry. And he asked himself why he hadn't.

He didn't get an answer.

* * *

Alaina gazed at Rafaello's retreating figure, heart thudding. Memories were clamouring—memories of her brief but unforgettable time long ago with Rafaello, on that magical Caribbean island. For a moment she just stood there, almost faint with the aftershock of seeing Rafaello walk back into her life.

'Mummee!'

She gave a gasp. Joey was emerging from the rotating door into the hotel, his hand held by Ryan. The instant he was clear he tore free and hurtled towards the reception desk, little face alight with delight.

In horror, she felt the world turn in slow motion, paralysing her. She could not move—not an inch.

Joey reached the desk, placed his little hands on the edge, standing on tiptoes to see her, his smile beaming. But her eyes were not on him. They had gone, as if dragged by weights she could not counter, to the bank of elevators.

She saw Rafaello pause in the act of pressing the button to call one. Saw his hand drop away. Saw him turn around. Saw his eyes go to Joey, hear him cry out *'Mummee!'* again, in excited greeting.

Saw Rafaello's expression change. His body freeze.

Then Ryan reached her desk as well. 'Hi,' he said easily. 'Here he is.' He ruffled Joey's hair with familiar affection.

She couldn't reply. Was incapable of doing so—incapable of anything at all except standing there, chest crushed, breathing impossible.

Rafaello had started to move. But not into the elevator, whose doors were now sliding open. He was coming towards her. Towards Joey. His face had no expression.

For a second—a fleeting instant—Alaina's mind raced. She would imply that Ryan was Joey's father, greet him as such...*anything* to disguise the truth. But as her eyes dropped to Joey she knew that trying to pass him off as Ryan's son—Ryan so fair, so completely unlike Joey—would be impossible.

The evidence of Rafaello's paternity was in Joey's face. Incontestably visible. The dark hair, dark eyes, the shape of his face—all declared it. Oh, there was something of herself in him as well, but he was Rafaello's son. What use would it be to try and deny it?

And Rafaello's gaze was riveted on Joey. Frozen. His every feature pulled tight like a wire.

He reached the desk. Both Ryan and Joey turned to look at him. Ryan stepped away, assuming he was a hotel guest wanting to ask Alaina something. Joey dropped his hands from the edge of the desk, looking curiously at Rafaello but knowing, as Alaina had trained him to know, that when Mummy was working he was not to interrupt.

For one endless second Rafaello just went on looking at Joey. His face was expressionless. Completely and absolutely expressionless. Then his eyes flicked to Ryan. Dismissed him. They shifted again, refocussing on her like lasers.

'Perhaps,' he said, his voice as chillingly expressionless as his face and his eyes going back to Alaina, 'you would care to explain?'

The blood drained from Alaina's face.

Rafaello could feel his heart slugging in his chest, like hammers beating at him from the inside. But he paid no attention. Paid no attention to anything at all except what he had just seen.

'Well?' he prompted, in the same tight, taut voice.

Her face had paled. Gone white as a sheet.

He'd seen witnesses in court look like that, when their alibies were demolished, their lies uncovered.

Lies of commission…

Or lies of omission…

He felt emotion spike somewhere inside him, like the skewering thrust of a knife, but he blanked it. It was essential to do so. Essential to do what he was doing now. Keep his face without expression, his voice without inflection.

She did not answer him. Instead, she came around the desk, her face still chalk-white, and spoke to the man who was surely irrelevant to this situation.

'Ryan…' her voice was low '…could you take Joey into the café for a few moments? Let him have a diluted orange juice.' Then she was hunkering down to the little boy. 'Joey, darling, nip off with Ryan for five minutes.' She gave him a tight hug, and a kiss on his cheek. Then she straightened, casting another look at Ryan.

Rafaello saw the irrelevant man pause for a moment, exchange a look with Alaina, and then cheerfully take the little boy by the hand and say, 'Come on, Joey, let's get you an OJ!'

They headed off to the café that opened off the lobby at the opposite end from the elevators. Rafaello watched them go for a moment. He felt that knife-thrust inside him again. Sharper this time. More skewering. But still his face was expressionless. Then he turned back to Alaina. She was still as white as a sheet, and he could see a nerve working in her throat.

She'd moved slightly to address one of the young women further down the reception desk, and he heard her ask her to hold the fort for a few minutes.

Then she looked back at him. 'My office,' she said.

She walked into a room behind the reception desk, her gait jerky, her entire body as tense as steel.

Rafaello followed her.

Closed the office door behind him.

Confronted the woman who had lied to him.

Lied to him for five years…

'He's mine.'

Alaina heard the words. They were quite expressionless. Her eyes went to Rafaello and she swallowed. Every muscle in her body was strained. Her throat tight.

'No,' she said, 'he's mine. Joey is my son.'

Did something move in his eyes? Those dark, lidded, completely expressionless eyes? She didn't now—knew only that the office had suddenly become stifling, suffocating. He dominated it. Dominated the room. Dominated everything.

But not me.

She could feel rebellion inside her. Resistance. Her eyes met his, full-on.

'Joey is my son, Rafaello,' she said again.

Her voice was steady, and she was proud of it, because it was costing her everything to keep it so. She took a breath—a careful one, because her lungs felt drained of oxygen.

'When we parted,' she went on, 'five years ago, it was a permanent parting after a very temporary affair. I knew that then. I have known it ever since. I know it now, still. You had no further interest in me and I accepted that. What became of my life thereafter was not your concern.' She paused. 'It still isn't.'

She saw something flash in his eyes, but it was so

fast it was soon gone, like a lightning bolt. She went on, doggedly trying to keep her voice steady, ignoring the tremor in it.

'I'm sorry this has happened. It's a shock to you. It's something I would never have imposed on you. My lack of contact these past five years must indicate that to you.'

She swallowed. There seemed to be a brick in her throat, but she swallowed all the same.

'I ask only that you…withdraw from the situation.'

Those lidded, expressionless eyes were still holding hers.

'Is Ryan your partner?' His brows drew together momentarily. 'Your husband?'

With all her heart Alaina wished she could give an answer that would protect her. But she shook her head.

'We help each other out with childcare. Nursery pickups and so on. He's divorced and has a little girl Joey's age he shares custody of. He's…a friend.'

'Good.'

The single monosyllable fell from his lips. It was as uninflected as anything else he'd addressed to her. Yet something seemed to ease across his shoulders—some of the stiffness, the tension she could see, the shock which, in fairness, he was entitled to feel.

But that was absolutely nothing to the thunderbolt of shock that slayed her at his next words.

'So there will be no impediment to our marriage, then,' he said.

CHAPTER TWO

RAFAELLO HEARD HER GASP. Saw the colour that had drained from her face suddenly shoot back in. Saw her eyes widen as if she could not believe what he had just said. Heard her voice echo his.

'Marriage?'

His mouth tightened. Somewhere, very deep within him, controlled with absolute insistence, something was moving. He would not acknowledge it. Would not permit it. Would deal only with what had to be dealt with right now.

'Just so,' he said.

Her eyes flared. Those expressive eyes that had always been so much a part of her beauty. But her beauty was irrelevant. There was one focus now. Only one.

'Are you mad?' She stared at him disbelievingly.

He gave a quick, impatient shake of his head.

'Prevarication is without purpose,' he answered. 'Do not waste my time contesting me.'

He paused, with purpose. The dark, subterranean emotions that were scything through him were strengthening, but he must continue to control them. Must make clear straight away the inevitable conclusion of the situation that had just presented itself like a bullet to his head, requiring an immediate decision.

'Neither now, nor...' he paused again, to drive his message home '...in court.'

Her face froze again.

'Court?'

He looked at her for a moment. Looked into the pallor of her whitened face.

'For five years,' he said, 'you have had my son. Now I will have him too...'

Alaina heard him speak, but his voice seemed to be coming from a long, long way away. Shock was still going through her—shock after shock after shock.

She felt herself sway...

A hand shot out, gripped her arm.

'Don't pass out on me, Alaina. There is no need.'

For the first time, through the mist that seemed to be rolling in all around her, she heard in his voice something akin to expression. Then she felt herself pressed down, a chair placed beneath her. She sank down on to it with nerveless legs that were suddenly jelly.

'Put your head down...let the blood get to your brain.'

The grip on her arm was released and of its own volition her head sank. Slowly the drumming eased, the mist rolled away. Heavily, she lifted her head.

He was looking down at her. He seemed different now. She didn't know how, or why, but he was. His voice was different too.

'Alaina, we can and shall be civilised about this. But you will need to co-operate with me. I have no wish— none!—to resort to legal proceedings, but please believe me that I will do so if you do not accept that we must now marry. I will give you time to accept that necessity but not a great deal.'

She gazed up at him blankly. Watched as he calmly sat himself down on another chair, and got his phone out of his jacket pocket, crossing one long leg over the other.

'There is a considerable exchange of information we must make, but we shall begin with the essentials.' He flicked his phone on, ready to tap in information. 'Let's start with your address.'

Rafaello lay on his hotel bed, looking up at the ceiling. There was a lot to get done and he needed to stay focussed. Absently, as if detaching part of his mind from the rest of it, he wondered how he was staying so calm. But he knew how. He had, instinctively, automatically, gone into the mode he adopted when he was being his professional self, and was treating what had happened this evening in the same dispassionate, forensic way. Analysing the situation swiftly, reaching the necessary conclusions, cutting to the chase, disposing of anything unnecessary.

Such as how he must process the information that had been thrust upon him a bare few hours earlier—the existence of a child, concealed from him, for whatever reason, by a woman he had assumed would never cross his path again.

He pulled his mind away from what did not matter right now to what did. To what he had spelt out to her with brutal but essential bluntness, ensuring the message hit home. He started to work his way mentally down the list of things that needed to be done. To be put in order. To be set to rights.

The same emotion that had scythed through him earlier swept its cutting blade through his chest again, extinguishing his breathing momentarily. For a timeless moment it demanded attention, demanded that he acknowledge it—acknowledge its existence and the reason for its existence. With an effort, but with ruthless self-discipline, he defied it.

This is not the occasion.

Then it passed, leaving him back in control. He returned to listing all the things that needed to be done. That neither he nor Alaina had any choice about.

Alaina lay huddled in her bed, duvet pulled tight around her, trying to shut what had happened out of her head. The disaster that had befallen her.

She would have given so much to have had it not happen. Not now.

Five years ago I had to choose—and I've stuck by that choice.

She had resisted, though it had cost her so much strength to do so, the overwhelming temptation to let Rafaello know that their affair had resulted in her pregnancy. It would have given her a means to call him back into her life. But she had known, brutally and inescapably, that he would not welcome the news.

He didn't want me, and he certainly would not have wanted a baby.

That was the blunt reality that had shaped her life since then. That had made her a single working mother, juggling her career and her baby, now an adored child, to give him the best life she could.

But now...

Now a question was pounding in her head—had been pounding ever since Rafaello had informed her he would be calling on her the following evening, to take matters further, then got to his feet and walked out of the office.

She'd sat there numbly for a moment, then jerked to her feet, hurrying out into the lobby. *Was he going to find Joey?* Fear—or an emotion something like fear—had clutched at her, but he had simply been striding towards the elevators and in a moment had disappeared.

Hurriedly, she'd dashed into the hotel's café, where Joey had been happily finishing his orange juice. Ryan had looked up as Alaina came in, and in his face had been an open question. She hadn't said anything, not with Joey there. She'd dropped a kiss on Joey's head, desperately trying to be normal, sound normal.

'All ready, poppet? Good, then let's say goodnight to Ryan and we can be off very soon. I just need to sort a couple of things, and then we'll get going.'

The three of them had gone back out into the lobby. At the hotel door Ryan had said quietly to her, 'I'm here if you need—'

She'd shaken her head instinctively. His concern had been obvious, but what could she have said to him? That a bomb had just exploded in her life, shattering her into pieces?

He'd patted her arm, his gesture sympathetic, and taken his leave.

Somehow she'd got through the business of handing over to her replacement, getting Joey, very tired by then, back home and into bed. In her head, circling like vultures, Rafaello's chill, expressionless words had gone round and round and round in tighter circles, tighter and tighter. They were circling still.

'Do not waste my time contesting me. Neither now nor in court.'

Oh, God, would he do that? Fear stabbed her.

What am I going to do? Dear God, what am I going to do?

The question echoed in her head. Finding no answer.

Rafaello's taxi pulled up at a small, modern semi-detached house in a quiet, tree-lined road on the residential edge of the town closest to the airport and he got out. He'd been busy that day. Very busy. He'd gone into London, had his meeting with his client, cancelled his homeward flight, changed his room reservation to an open-ended stay, then started the process of checking UK law on disputed child custody and the fastest way to marry.

Alaina could take her choice. He would allow no other.

He set that out plainly to her as he sat himself down in the compact but comfortable modestly appointed sitting room.

Tension was racking through her—that was obvious enough. She sat perched on the sofa opposite his armchair, hands clasped tightly in her lap so that the knuckles showed white. Though his own habitually well-schooled demeanour displayed no tension, he was aware that it was present all the same.

But how could it not be, given the revelation that had ripped into his life twenty-four hours ago? Tearing it apart...

'So, what decision have you come to?' he asked.

His eyes rested on her. She was pale, but not as ghost-white as she'd been the night before. Her hair was still drawn back off her face, and she wore not a scrap of make-up. She was wearing long black trousers and a dark green polo-neck jumper emphasised her pallor.

In spite of that, her beauty was undimmed.

He could feel it drawing him—just as it had five years ago, when he had first seen her, catching his lingering eye as she sunned herself on the beach. But he pulled his wayward thoughts to heel. It had been her beauty then, her allure for him, that had resulted in this situation. The situation which must hold his sole focus—without the distraction of recognising that her beauty was undimmed. That did not matter—he would not allow it to.

He gave himself an admonishing mental shake. All that mattered was that upstairs his son was sleeping—the son who, a bare twenty-four hours earlier, he had not even known existed. Emotion came again, slicing through him—that same dark, unnameable emotion that had scythed through him last night as he had taken on board the realisation of what had been hidden from him, deliberately and determinedly.

But this was no time for indulging in emotions. They only made for confusion and conflict. It was a lesson he'd learnt early in life. His father had been very clear about the importance of that lesson. Life ran far more smoothly without excessive emotion getting in the way.

So now he would apply that hard-earned knowledge. Would resolve matters as swiftly and as expediently as necessary. He had given Alaina a clear choice. Now she must make it.

'Well?' he prompted.

He saw her swallow, lick her lips—and ignored the flicker inside him that the unconscious gesture caused. That, too, was utterly irrelevant to the situation. His keen legal mind would allow no distractions, no deviations.

He saw her hands clench more tightly. She swallowed again, then spoke.

'Before…before I answer you, you must tell me why… why you want anything to do with…'

'With my son?' He completed her sentence, unable to keep the edge out of his voice. 'The answer is in the very statement. *My son.*'

Something flared in her eyes. Fear, or rejection, or protest. He didn't know. Didn't care.

'But *why*? What we had—it was a holiday romance! You said as much. You made it crystal-clear you didn't want anything more!'

'No,' he answered. 'I didn't.' Truthful. Brutal. But protecting her feelings right now was not his priority. 'But I want my son.'

'*Why?*'

The word was wrung from her. He looked across at her.

'Why do *you* want him?' he countered.

Her face contorted. 'That's a stupid question!'

'No more stupid than you asking me.' He could hear the edge back in his voice, like a honed blade. 'I want him.'

'But you've had nothing to do with him! You don't know him. You're a stranger—a complete stranger!'

That nameless emotion scythed through him again, more powerfully this time, and this time he could not bank it down. His mouth thinned, like a whip.

'You sit there, having kept my son from me, kept from me all knowledge of him, and presume to say that to me?' He held up a hand. Peremptory. Impatient. As when a witness attempted to prevaricate. 'Alaina, you will believe me on this, if nothing else. I am my son's father. I have responsibilities that come with that. Responsibilities I have no intention of reneging on. I will be part of his life, as his father. All that is to be decided is whether we do this the civil way…or the uncivil. I can't tell you which to choose—only you can do that. So…choose.'

He paused.

'Custody battles can be vicious, expensive and destructive. And…' his voice changed '…unnecessary.'

He paused again, not letting her eyes drop from his. When he spoke his voice had changed again.

'The alternative,' he said, 'is what I will outline to you.'

He drew a breath. Her hands were still clutched together, knuckles still white. There was tension in every line of her body, her face drawn and pale. He made his voice calm, composed, unemotional. Setting out the situation the same way he did with his clients.

'If you agree to a marriage between us,' he said, spelling it out, his voice neutral, his expression likewise, 'it will be on the following lines. We make a civil marriage in as short a time as the law allows. You resign from your job. You travel with me, with our son, and you come to live in Italy with me. I will provide a suitable home, and our marriage will be civilised and without hostility. You will accept the situation as it must be.'

He paused again, his gaze resting steadily, unreadably, on her. 'Is that not a less destructive option?'

He saw her shut her eyes, shake her head slowly. But not in rejection. More in exhaustion. Her head drooped.

Rafaello surveyed her. Long experience usually told him when his point had been taken. When his goal had been achieved. His eyes rested on her. Memory mixed with the present moment. Conflating. Confusing.

He did not care for confusion. He required clarity at all times. Clarity and control. Or chaos ensued.

Her eyes opened, meeting his. She was making them meet his, he could see.

He spoke again and his voice was conciliatory. Collusive, even.

'Alaina, whatever my opinion on whether you should have told me our affair had left you pregnant, you made the decision you did. Now that I know about my son, however, you must decide again. I would infinitely prefer not to go down the ugly route that leads to a courtroom, which is why I will argue in favour of the alternative I have put to you.'

He paused for a moment, letting her absorb what he was telling her, just as he did with his clients, getting them to accept what they might not wish to, but what the law would insist on.

He was insisting now. But his tone of voice was still conciliatory as he picked up his speech again. Her hostility would not be helpful—would only hinder the outcome that he wished to achieve.

'If it helps you accept it, consider that this need not be permanent. For a young child, a stable home with both parents provides the most secure childhood. But...'

Even as he spoke memory burned in him, like a cigarette being extinguished on his skin. Had his own childhood been secure, for all the married status of his ill-matched parents? In his head he could hear his mother's weeping voice, calling in anguish to her husband, could see his father dislodging her clinging hands, walking out of the room in stiff, exasperated strides. Then he saw his mother, stooping down, face ravaged by tears, clutching him to her, still weeping hysterically. His own body had been as stiff and tense as his father's...

He thrust the memory from him. Whatever this marriage he now had to make would be, he would ensure it was nothing like his parents'. It would be calm, and civilised, and emotion would be completely unnecessary.

His mouth compressed for a moment and then he continued, setting the scene for this woman who had, without any intention on his part, borne him a son.

'But an older child, able to express his own views in a rational way, would have no objection to us divorcing and making our own individual lives again. That is for the future—but bear it in mind as you make your decision now.'

He paused for a moment, letting the information be absorbed. Then he spoke again, his voice as calm as ever.

'Give me your answer tomorrow. Then I will make the appropriate arrangements—whatever they are to be.'

She lifted her head, looked at him without expression. Closed in on herself.

'You know,' she said. 'You already know what those arrangements will be. You have spelt it out to me. A custody battle would be hideous and—' he saw her mouth twist '—what kind of lawyer could I possibly afford to stand against you?'

Something moved in her eyes—an expression he could not read. Then she said, with emphasis in her voice, 'I would never, *never* put Joey through that! Anything has to be better than that. *Anything!*'

He gave a slow, considered nod. Her face was still pale, her tension unabated.

'I am glad that is how you see it,' he said. He paused, then spoke again. 'Alaina, understand that my responsibility for my son is absolute—as is yours. Our decisions can only be based on that.'

He got to his feet, moved to the door of the sitting room.

'I'll take my leave—don't see me out.'

He walked out of the room. As he passed the staircase his glance went upwards. Somewhere up there the son of whose existence he had had no idea was sleeping…

Once again that scything of emotion cut through him. Then, with a quickening stride, he let himself out, climbing into the taxi he'd ordered to wait by the kerb, and was gone.

Alaina sat on the floor beside Joey's little bed. He was fast asleep, teddy clasped to him. Her heart was heavy, and she was hearing again Rafaello's voice in her head—but from long ago. Five years ago.

'I'm sorry if you've read more into our time together than there has been in reality. Perhaps the island is to blame—palm trees and silver sand and a tropical moon can send the wrong messages.'

Was that all it had been? The working of the moon on the sea? The gentle soughing of the warm breeze in the fronded palms? The soft sand beneath her feet as they'd walked along the midnight beach? The velvet seduction of his mouth on hers as he took her into his arms? Had it only been the romance of the place that had made her so susceptible to him? That had made her want to chuck in her job, be whisked back to Rome with him, to want her time with him to go on and on…?

Because Rafaello was a man like no other she had known. She had known that vividly, from the very start. Oh, the setting out in the Caribbean had helped—she acknowledged that—but that was not the reason she had been so smitten. It was Rafaello himself.

From the moment she'd glanced up from her sunbathing to find herself being leisurely, appreciatively perused by a tall, good-looking, sable-haired man strolling along the beach from the Falcone hotel next door. His lean, fit body had been displayed very nicely by dark green shorts and an open-fronted moss-green short-sleeved cotton shirt. His eyes had been shaded by designer shades, making him look—she'd gulped silently—darkly glamorous and enticing.

From that very moment she'd been hooked. When she'd encountered him again, the following evening, going across to the Falcone with some off-duty colleagues to the famous weekly barbecue there, she had not made the slightest objection when he'd singled her out and, with effortless ease, taken her off to share a quiet coffee and liqueur with him on the far side of the crowded pool and barbecue area.

It was all that had proved necessary. His eyes, his attentions… All had told her he found her desirable. And she… Oh, she had found him even more so…

She had gone along with his skilled, effortless seduction with full, enraptured co-operation. Giving herself entirely to the romance of it all. Snatching every moment she could to be with him. Knowing, instinctively, powerfully, irresistibly, that this was a romance like no other…knowing how very, very close she was to falling in love with him…

She had known, above all, that had he asked her to stay with him she'd have given only one answer. Known she was standing on the edge of the very cliff her mother had warned her of.

'Be careful…oh, so careful, my darling daughter! Do not give your heart to someone who does not want it—as I have done.'

But she had pulled back from the edge of that cliff just in time. Saved herself from her mother's heartbreak.

Rafaello had not asked her to stay with him.

Yet now he was demanding just that—because of Joey.

There was an irony in it somewhere—one that had an edge to it. A sharp and cutting edge.

She got to her feet, still looking down at Joey, sleeping so peacefully. In the morning, his life would change for ever—and there was absolutely nothing she could do about it. And her life would change for ever too. She would uproot herself, give up her job, leave her little house, the friends she'd made, leave her familiar life to move a thousand miles away, settle in a foreign land. And there was absolutely nothing she could do about that either...

And, since there was nothing she could do about it, she shut her eyes for a moment. What else could she do but accept it?

Nothing...nothing at all.

Slowly, she opened her eyes again, looked down at her precious son, sleeping so peacefully. Her heart was full, and heavy, as she walked quietly from the room.

CHAPTER THREE

RAFAELLO STEPPED OUT of the taxi that had just pulled up outside Alaina's house. This time it was morning, not evening. This time there was no confrontation awaiting him. Alaina had yielded to what was the only sane and reasonable outcome for the situation in which they both found themselves.

But even if there was no confrontation, what *was* awaiting him brought far more tension. He would be meeting his son.

For a second, blankness descended on him. What did he know of fatherhood? Nothing. It was a skill he'd never required. Never contemplated or thought about. But now he must.

How do I do this?

The question was blunt and stark, and memory flashed suddenly—unbidden and unwelcome. His father. Shooting a frowning, displeased look at him, telling him brusquely to lower his voice, enquiring acidly whether he had completed the assignments set by his school for the summer holidays… Then making some crushing reply to his mother, who had immediately protested, telling him something about the holidays being for relaxation and enjoyment. Then walking out of the room, his displeasure evident, back to his study, where no one was permitted to disturb him.

He thrust the memory away. Whatever kind of father he made for the son whose existence he had just discovered, he would not be harsh, like his own father. Never that.

I will do my best by him.

Whatever that 'best' was.

His expression set. After all, wasn't he prepared to give up the life he had enjoyed immensely till now? Give up his freedom, his comfortable, self-considering existence, to marry, to change his life completely, change his way of living? He would do that for his son, unhesitatingly, unflinchingly.

Resolved—steeled—he pressed the doorbell.

'Joey, darling, there's someone I want you to meet.'

The doorbell had just rung and Joey had looked up from his train set, which he was laying out on the sitting room floor with Alaina. She got up and went to the front door, conscious of a tightening in her lungs, a rise in her heart rate.

Rafaello, on schedule, was standing there. Dressed in the same charcoal-grey suit with its immaculate Italian tailoring, his shirt pristine, his silk tie stylish but understated, a brief glint of gold from his cufflinks. A completely irrelevant kick went through her at the impact he made, but she stifled it.

Rafaello greeted her coolly, and she made herself answer in the same way. Yet for all his self-contained composure she was aware of a tension in him that mirrored her own. Well, that was hardly surprising…

She led him into the sitting room.

Joey looked interestedly at him. 'You're the man at the hotel,' he announced.

Alaina saw Rafaello nod gravely. She was standing slightly to one side, and she could feel her already elevated heart rate racking up a notch.

'Yes, I am,' Rafaello said. 'And you are Joey.'

'Hello,' said Joey. He cocked his head to one side. 'I am playing with my trains,' he informed Rafaello.

'So you are,' Rafaello agreed, in the same grave manner.

Alaina could see a nerve working at his cheekbone, but he gave no other sign that he was, for the very first time in his life, talking to the son he had never known existed.

A shadow passed over her face.

Did I do the right thing, keeping Joey's existence from him?

It was a troubling thought—and a familiar one. She had struggled with it all through her pregnancy, and the decision not to tell Rafaello, to make no contact with him, had not been an easy one. She felt her chest tighten painfully. Now the struggle was over—whether she liked it or not.

Rafaello knew about Joey.

Knew about him. Wanted him. Was determined to have him, whatever it took.

Even to the point of marrying her.

She felt a lump inside her, hard and heavy. Five years ago, had Rafaello asked her to marry him, had he swept her off her feet and back to Italy, she'd have thrown herself into his arms and been carried off by him in a state of romantic bliss, a whirlwind of longing fulfilled...

Now it was different. So very, very different.

Joey was telling Rafaello about his trains. Rafaello had an attentive expression on his face. The two faces were so alike in appearance. She watched them both, her emotions confused. Father and son…

'Won't you sit down?' She gestured to the sofa.

'Thank you,' said Rafaello, still speaking gravely, and did so.

His tall figure seemed to dwarf the small sofa, as it had the previous night, when he'd given her the option of marrying him or fighting him for custody.

She felt emotion churn within her—and not all of it was on account of that impossible choice. As her gaze went to Rafaello, she felt again the impact of his presence. Again, she pushed it aside. She must not dwell on how her gaze wanted to drink him in, must not conjure memories, nor allow emotions that had no place.

I banished them a long, long time ago. I let them wither and die, and never gave them air or light to breathe and survive.

And it was essential—utterly essential—that she never let herself remember her time with him. It would serve no purpose. The only purpose was Joey.

She took a breath, hunkering down beside him on the carpet.

'Joey, darling, there's something I must tell you.' She took one of his little hands in his. Took another breath, conscious of how tight her throat suddenly was. 'This is your *papà*, Joey. Your daddy. Like Ryan is Betsy's daddy.'

Joey's gaze went to Rafaello, open and direct as only a child's could be.

'Hello,' he said. Then he frowned. 'Why were you not here before?' he asked.

Alaina felt her throat constrict even more. Oh, dear God…out of the mouths of babes and innocents…

Her eyes flew to Rafaello. What would he say? Panic beat briefly.

'I have been abroad, Joey,' Rafaello said calmly. 'I live in Italy. And now,' he said, in the same matter-of-fact manner, 'you and your mother are going to be coming to live with me there too.'

Joey's gaze had gone back to Alaina. 'Are we, Mummy?' he asked for confirmation.

She nodded, her throat still tight. 'Yes,' she said. 'It will be fun.'

He looked at her consideringly, then at Rafaello, then back at Alaina. 'Can I bring my trains?' he asked. 'And all my toys?'

'Yes,' said Rafaello.

'Good,' said Joey.

That, it seemed, was all he needed to know. He went back to laying out the track, talking to his trains and answering back for them as he moved them along the track.

Rafaello got quietly to his feet, and Alaina stood up too.

'Would…would you like a coffee?' she asked, not quite knowing what to do or say now.

She led the way into the kitchen—Joey would be happy for a while now, occupied with his train set. Rafaello followed her, perching himself on a stool by the narrow breakfast bar.

She busied herself putting on the kettle. 'It's only instant,' she apologised.

'Fa niente,' he answered.

She swallowed. 'That…that seems to have gone off… well,' she said. 'Maybe children just…just accept things.'

'As we must too,' Rafaello replied.

She nodded, went back to measuring the coffee into mugs. 'What happens now?' she asked.

She was being very calm and was grateful for it. Maybe staying calm, not letting emotions cloud and confuse and upset her—emotions for which there was no place, surely?—was the best or rather least worst way of coping?

Rafaello was being calm, cool and dispassionate—and she would be too. Somehow it made this entire unreal situation less…

Less real?

She felt her heart rate quicken, adrenaline starting to run. How could she possibly be standing here, making coffee for a man who'd told her she must marry him or face a custody battle for her beloved son? A man she hadn't seen for five years? A man she'd never thought to see again…?

How unreal is this? Totally, totally unreal!

Except that it wasn't—and she had to deal with it, process it, adopt a façade, at the very least, of being as calm as he was as they coolly discussed the practicalities of what was going to change their lives for ever.

He was answering her, and she dragged her wayward mind back to what he was saying.

'Paperwork,' came his reply. 'Setting in motion the necessities required for our marriage. Does Joey have a passport?'

'Yes. We went to France on the Eurostar last Christmas, with Ryan and Betsy.'

Rafaello's face suddenly hardened. Alaina pre-empted what was obviously going to be his next question. 'I told you—he's just a friend. In France he shared with Betsy and I shared with Joey. We went to the big theme parks just outside Paris—the children were over the moon.'

Even as she explained, she felt resentful. Why should she defend herself? Even had she wanted an affair with

Ryan—had she wanted more than an affair—what business would it be of Rafaello's?

He didn't want me. He made that clear.

Just as he was making it crystal-clear it was Joey he wanted now, not her...

She made herself say it in her head. That, and nothing more, was to be the basis of their marriage. The reason for it. Nothing else.

We'll just be Joey's parents—that's all. Nothing else...

She shut down her thoughts. She was coping as best she could. Forty-eight hours earlier her life had been what it had been for the last five years. Now it was turned upside down. She would cope only by taking one step at a time. Looking no further than that.

It's all I can deal with.

She filled his coffee mug, placed it in front of him. He drank it black, she remembered. But then there was such a lot she remembered about him...

She pulled her thoughts away. Back to something she wanted him to tell her.

'What is Joey to call you? I mean... Dad, or Daddy, or something in Italian? What?'

'Papà will be fine,' Rafaello said.

She nodded, pouring milk into her own coffee.

'He will need to learn Italian,' Rafaello went on. 'You as well—it would be helpful.'

'OK,' she said. 'Joey will probably pick it up faster than I will—they are like sponges at that age. I'm sure he'll be speaking it in no time.'

A sudden convulsion went through her. It showed in her face, she knew, but she could not stop it. This was not the childhood she had thought Joey would have—being taken from his home to another country, having to learn that language, taking the nationality of his father...the father who didn't know him at all.

And why is that?

The question stabbed at her, but she stabbed back.

I had to make that call! I had to decide whether a man who had made it crystal-clear I was a holiday romance only would regard his son's existence as anything but an unwelcome nuisance. Would wish he didn't exist at all.

But she couldn't and wouldn't rehash that argument. Nor was there any point in doing so. It was the present she had to deal with—not the past. Rafaello had walked back into her life. She had never thought he would, but he had. And he'd announced that he wanted a role in Joey's life.

He was going to have one.

And that was all there was to it.

So there are no more decisions for me to make. I'm going along with this because the alternative would be a nightmare I could not endure and could never risk.

She dropped her eyes to her coffee, mechanically stirring in the milk. A question was stirring in her head as well. A question she didn't want to ask—let alone answer.

But what are you risking this way?

She thrust it away. Refusing to heed it.

The taxi was back yet again, outside Alaina's house, but this time Rafaello was not going in. She was coming out. And when she did it would be to lock the door after her and leave her life in England behind.

She will join her life to mine.

It was not the way he'd intended the years ahead to play out, but necessity—in the form of their son—required it. And Alaina, too, acknowledged that necessity. Accepted the necessity of their marriage as composedly and dispassionately as he did—for that he was decidedly appreciative.

He shut his eyes for a moment, felt memories of his own childhood pressing in again. His mother's endless out-of-control emotion, her hysteria as his father coldly condemned it, always weeping and wailing…

What if the woman he was having to marry was anything like that?

He felt an inner shudder, followed by a sense of relief.

We shall make it as good a marriage as circumstances permit. We will primarily be parents, make a stable home for our son.

Anything else…

He felt his mind shy away. Anything else would be dealt with as and when it occurred. It was not necessary to think about it now.

Through the taxi window he saw her emerge and lock the door behind her. She stood, just for a moment, looking at the house she owned. The house she was leaving. Then, with a straightening of her shoulders, she turned and walked towards the taxi at the kerb, pulling her cabin bag with her. Their main luggage had been air-freighted out that week, was now awaiting her in Rome.

They would marry that afternoon, collect Joey from nursery, then fly out to Italy. Their marriage would begin today.

That was all there was to it. It was necessary, and it would be done.

He stepped out, went to relieve her of her cabin bag, usher her into the taxi. She was pale, but calm, wearing her business suit, her hair neat in its French plait, her make-up minimal.

A frown of sudden displeasure crossed Rafaello's face.

Whatever their priorities in Italy, one priority was clear. She must dress according to her role as his wife. Displeasure turned to a glint in his eyes. Playing down her beauty, as she now did, would no longer be required.

He shook off the thought. That was for later. For now, there was a wedding to get through.

He turned to her. 'Ready?' he asked.

Did her fingers tighten over her handbag? He wasn't sure. But her voice was calm, if taut, as she answered him.

'Yes,' she said.

It was all that was necessary for him to hear.

The taxi moved off. Taking them to their wedding.

Alaina stood beside Rafaello in the register office. Other than a floral display on the table, there was no sign that something as celebratory as a wedding was taking place. Rafaello was wearing a business suit and so was she— she'd finished her last shift at the hotel that morning, and her employment there. Joey was at nursery. His last day too.

They would be flying out to Italy after this brief but legally binding ceremony made her Rafaello's wife.

To begin their new life there.

In the weeks that had passed since Rafaello had discovered the existence of Joey, Alaina felt—in so far as she was allowing herself to feel anything at all—she had come to passively accept what was going to happen now. In that she had been helped by Rafaello's own attitude, and she found herself mirroring it. It was the simplest way to deal with the situation. He was calm, composed and matter-of-fact. So was she.

That matter-of-fact attitude was good for Joey, too.

If he sees me accepting what is happening, then so will

*he. He seems, in his simple, childlike way, to have ac-
cepted Rafaello's appearance in his life. And if Joey can
accept him—so can I.*

Because this marriage she was making—entering into
right at this very moment—had nothing to do with her or
with Rafaello. It had nothing to do with what had once
been between them—with what she had wanted and he
had not. It had nothing to do with her having once stood
so close to the brink of falling in love with Rafaello—or
with the fact that she had pulled back just in time when
he'd returned to Italy. It had nothing to do with their feelings, or what they themselves wanted or might want.

It was for Joey's sake. That was all.

Only Joey.

And that, she knew, as she stood there giving the responses the registrar required, speaking in a voice that
was as calm and composed as Rafaello's as he gave his
own responses, was what was going to make it possible
for her to make this marriage work.

Joey was gazing out of the window at the Rome traffic,
but was too sleepy to take in any of it. He'd enjoyed the
flight over, asking Rafaello endless questions, which had
been patiently answered—from why the plane didn't fall
out of the sky to why the packet of unopened crisps had
gone so puffy.

Alaina had been glad to leave them to it, staring
blankly out of the window at the white cloudscape beyond. Now, leaning back in the luxurious interior of the
chauffeured car into which Rafaello had ushered them at
the airport, she felt thoughts circling in her mind, slow
and incomprehensible.

This is my wedding day...

But it was best not to dwell on that. Better to focus only on practicalities, as she had ever since she had accepted the choice Rafaello had put before her.

Landing in Italy had brought home to her just how much she was changing her life. It had made her glad that she had laid down some stipulations of her own. Joey would keep his British citizenship, and so would she. Her passport was still in her own name, and his too. She would keep her house, bought with an inheritance from her late mother. She would keep her own credit cards and bank accounts, and all her financial affairs—such as they were— would remain hers.

Whatever she was to become as Rafaello's wife, she would remain who she was as well. Rafaello had made no demur at all, and she was glad of that too.

His words came back to her now.

'We can do this—we can make a civil, civilised marriage.'

And that was what they would do. She drew a breath, fingers tightening over her handbag. Yes, a civil, civilised marriage. It could be done. It must be done. It *would* be done.

'We're nearly there.' Rafaello's low voice penetrated her thoughts. 'My apartment is in an old nineteenth-century mansion in the *centro storico*. As we discussed, it will be our base for now, but Joey will want more space, so we'll take a house outside the city as well. Finding something suitable will be a priority.'

She nodded, and when a short time later she stood in the elegant surroundings of Rafaello's apartment, she could see how it was not an ideal home for Joey. Occupying the *piano nobile* of the grand old house, with a cobbled inner courtyard its only outdoor space, it was furnished with antiques and displayed what she suspected were very expensive *objets d'art*. Not at all appropriate for a lively four-year-old.

Not that Joey was lively at the moment, leaning against her half asleep and yawning.

Rafaello showed them into a bedroom where a truckle bed had been set up next to a beautiful carved one swathed in a richly embroidered counterpane that she swiftly removed and folded to place safely in the equally beautiful carved wardrobe.

Then, focussing on getting Joey to bed, she led him into the en suite bathroom, as opulent as the bedroom, and gave him a very cursory 'up and down' flannel wash. She whisked him into his pyjamas, and tucked him into the truckle bed with his beloved Mr Teds clutched to him. He was asleep in moments.

She stood looking down at him, her heart feeling strange. For the sake of this so beloved child she had uprooted herself from everything that was familiar, from the life she had painstakingly made for herself. Had committed to a marriage that felt more unreal than anything else...

She bent to bestow a swift, emotional kiss upon Joey's forehead, a wave of love welling out from her.

I can do this! I can do this for you, my darling boy! And it will be all right! I promise you I will do everything to make it all right for you!

She straightened, still gazing down at him in the soft light from the bedside lamp on the far side of the other bed. Then, with a breath, she turned and left the room.

She found Rafaello waiting for her in the apartment's dining room. Beautifully draped dark green velvet curtains shaded the sash windows, and a polished mahogany table was set for two with silverware, crystal glasses and linen napery. For the first time it struck her that Rafaello Ranieri was a substantially wealthy man.

Oh, she had known that ever since their first encounter—no one staying at the Falcone, next door to the four-star hotel she'd worked at, could ever be anything other than wealthy. But he'd been on holiday, and it hadn't really registered. They'd dined out at expensive restaurants, true, and his clothes—even the beach casuals he'd worn—had clearly not come from chain stores, but for all that she'd paid little attention to his material circumstances.

Now, as he greeted her in his cool fashion, enquired after Joey and then invited her to take her place at the table, she glanced around her at the ultra-elegant apartment, at the antiques and *objets d'art*, at the old-fashioned landscape paintings on the walls that might as well have been in a museum, it was hitting home.

The emergence of a manservant through a service door only emphasised it.

Rafaello introduced her, and the middle-aged man bowed his head politely. He proceeded to beckon to a maid, who came forward with their *aperitivo*, then presented to Rafaello a bottle of wine from the marble-topped sideboard.

Carefully, Alaina spread a pristine linen napkin over her lap, hearing again Rafaello's introduction of her to his staff.

'This is Signora Ranieri.'

It was the first time she'd heard it, and she could feel a jolt of disbelief go through her.

'Alaina?'

Rafaello was indicating to her, asking whether she would care for wine. She nodded, and he poured her a glass. The maid was placing plates in front of them, and Alaina murmured her thanks. Then the staff left them to it and she was alone with Rafaello. The man she had married that afternoon for the sake of the little boy now fast asleep in that bedroom.

'I think,' Rafaello announced, 'we should drink a toast, Alaina.'

She saw him lift his glass, tilt it across the table towards her.

'To making this a successful marriage,' he said.

His voice was as cool as it ever was, but there was a strange expression in his dark eyes.

'We can do it, Alaina,' he said quietly. 'If we put our minds to it.'

She nodded numbly, lifting her own glass. She could not quite return his toast, but took a mouthful of the ruby liquid. It tasted rich, and expensive, and she hadn't the faintest idea what it was. But it went with the restrained elegance all around her—with the cool, composed man sitting opposite her, so good-looking in his austere way, with his slate-dark, long-lashed eyes and a sensual twist to his well-shaped mouth...

Out of nowhere, she felt danger lick at her. Danger... and memory.

She must permit neither. Not in a marriage like theirs.

She set down her glass with a click.

'Yes,' she said, 'I think we can.'

A faint smile curved his mouth and he lowered his glass, picking up his knife and fork to do justice to the buttered scallops on his plate, bathed in a saffron *jus*.

Alaina picked up her cutlery too, and started on her dinner.

The first meal of her new life with Rafaello.

Her husband.

It still felt completely and totally unreal.

CHAPTER FOUR

DESPITE HER ASSUMPTION to the contrary, Alaina slept well and dreamlessly. So did Joey—for which she was very grateful. He woke her, as he always did, by clambering into bed with her, Mr Teds clutched in one hand, and snuggling up to her.

'Morning, munchkin,' she greeted him drowsily.

His little body was strong, and warm, and precious to embrace.

'Are we on holiday?' he asked.

She smiled. 'It will feel like a holiday, yes,' she said. 'But it's a sort of adventure too.'

'I like adventures,' he replied happily.

Alaina was glad of his answer. Even if it only applied for now. The whole question of how he would adapt to the way his life would be now hung unanswered and un-answerable.

A piercing longing filled her to get a taxi to the airport, take the first flight home, back to the life she had made for herself these last five years.

But that life was gone.

It was this new one she had to get used to. And so did Joey.

She busied herself getting Joey up and dressing him in

cotton trousers and a checked shirt. She dressed herself in sleek black trousers and a lightweight knitted top, drew her hair back into her customary French plait. She was not bothering with make-up because there was no need for any. In the dining room, already seated, was Rafaello, surrounded by breakfast. He rose to his feet as she came in.

'*Buongiorno,*' he said, pleasantly enough.

His glance went to Joey. Did it change? Alaina couldn't tell. She was too preoccupied with controlling her own reaction to seeing Rafaello, feeling that kick in her pulse coming again. Would she get used to it? Well, she must—that was all, she resolved.

The novelty will wear off before long.

That was the way to think of it. She was not letting him get to her.

He wasn't paying attention to her at the moment, and that was good at least. He pulled out a chair beside him, already supplied with a booster seat, and Joey trotted forward enthusiastically, clambering up, as Alaina took another chair. Three breakfast places had been laid, and on the table was a jug of orange juice, a pot of coffee, hot milk, and a generous basket of delicious-looking bread rolls and pastries, with pats of butter, jam and honey.

'Yummy!' said Joey, eyeing it all in a pleased fashion.

Alaina poured some orange juice for him, diluting it with iced water from a jug also on the table, then buttering one of the bread rolls for him.

'Bread roll first, then you can have one of the croissants,' she told him.

'In Italy, croissants are called *cornetti*,' said Rafaello.

'Like ice-cream cornets,' said Joey, looking at him.

'Yes, because both are horn-shaped, and "horn" is the root Latin word,' supplied Rafaello.

'What is Latin?' Joey asked, biting into his bread roll.

'It is the language spoken by the ancestors of the Italians—the Romans. The Romans lived very long ago, and ruled Europe, and many of the words they used we still find in our languages today. Like cornet and *cornetti*.'

Alaina sat quietly, pouring herself some orange juice and then a cup of strong, aromatic coffee, which she diluted with hot milk.

Memory struck her: breakfasting with Rafaello on the balcony of his room at the Falcone, sunshine blazing on the azure sea, her wrapped in the cotton bathrobe that came with the room, Rafaello in a grey silk knee-length dressing gown, its wide lapels showing his smooth chest, long legs stretched out, both of them languorous from their morning lovemaking...

She snapped the memory shut. That was then. This was now. And there were five long years in between.

Her eyes dropped to her son, munching on his bread roll while his father told him more about the Romans and he listened interestedly.

All that links me to Rafaello is Joey—nothing else.

That was what she must remember. She was here, back in Rafaello's smooth, ordered life, simply because there had been a failure of contraception. An accident. Unintended...unintentional.

She felt her heart contract as her eyes rested on Joey, her expression softening automatically. A wave of love so overwhelming it was almost unbearable dissolved her. Out of that 'accident' had come the most precious baby in all the world...the most beloved son.

And for his sake—only his—I am going to do anything! Anything at all for him!

Including what she had done yesterday.

Her eyes lifted to Rafaello, still talking with Joey. His face was unreadable.

Emotions, strange and inchoate, ebbed and flowed within her, making little sense.

But it didn't matter what she felt or didn't feel, nor that she couldn't work out what she was feeling. The die had been cast. Yesterday she had become the wife of Joey's father, and from now on that was what she must steer her course by.

Their discussion of the ancient Romans came to an end, with Joey diverted by finishing his buttered roll and remembering what she'd said about the *cornetti*. She gave her permission, and he helped himself to one, soon getting stuck in in a crumby sort of way.

She turned to Rafaello. 'What is to happen today?' she asked him.

He took a mouthful of his coffee. 'I plan on driving us out beyond the city. I have a shortlist of houses to view, and you can choose which you think most suitable.'

They set off on just that mission shortly after breakfast.

Joey, cleaned up from the stickiness he'd acquired over breakfast, happily climbed into the sleek saloon car waiting for them at the kerbside. Alaina took a moment to look about her at the cobbled *piazza*, lined by elegant, terraced mansions and sporting an ornate stone fountain in the centre, from which water was issuing sedately. The ambience was one of distinct but understated wealth.

It suited Rafaello, she thought.

'This apartment is very conveniently situated,' he said, dismissing the chauffeur as Alaina took her seat beside Joey and taking the wheel himself. 'A good base for when we are entertaining or going out by ourselves.'

'By ourselves?' Alaina spoke sharply.

'Whichever house outside the city you choose, it will be staffed,' Rafaello said. 'So there will always be care for Joey there. As my *wife*, Alaina,' he said, and his voice had changed, but she didn't quite know how, 'you will be required to do some socialising.'

She didn't answer, only settled Joey into his child seat. She wasn't sure what to make of what Rafaello had just announced.

Maybe I just haven't thought that far ahead.

She pushed it out of her mind as Rafaello drove off, and both she and Joey looked out of the windows with interest as they turned into a wider street and the vibrant city of Rome leapt into life. The traffic was appalling, and she made a comment to say so.

'Notorious!' he agreed. 'It's why I seldom drive myself. Being driven means I can get work done while stuck in traffic.'

It seemed a justifiable explanation for such luxury, but it was also, Alaina knew, another indication that Rafaello Ranieri was a wealthy man. She didn't know how wealthy and didn't much care. She knew only that he had the funds—and his own legal skill, of course—to mount a formidable custody challenge, should she have defied him about what had taken place yesterday at the register office.

She felt her hands tighten in her lap. Surely anything was better than that?

She shook the question from her. It was too late to have questions or doubts—the deed was done. Like it or not, she had uprooted her life—and Joey's—and now she was Signora Ranieri... Rafaello's wife. She took a quick breath. Whether it felt real or unreal made no difference to that truth whatsoever.

She just had to get on with it. With as good a grace as she could muster.

Rafaello paused at the exit of the driveway of the third house that Alaina had rejected and consulted the estate agent's list on his phone. Would the next house fare any better? She had rejected the first three on the grounds that they were too large, too grand and too formal.

'Isn't there anywhere more…well, *ordinary*?' she asked now.

He turned to look at her. 'Is that what you would prefer?' His voice was studiedly neutral.

'Yes,' she said.

'Very well.'

He set off again. The villa they were now heading for had not been in his top three, and it was a little further out from the city than he'd planned, but when they drove up to it Alaina smiled.

'Oh, but this is charming!' she exclaimed. Her voice was warm.

They got out of the car and he could see her looking about, her expression also warm. The narrow road beyond the stone wall girding the perimeter had been very quiet, and certainly there was no audible traffic here, only birdsong in the plentiful trees all about. The villa was Mediterranean in style but of indeterminate age, and it seemed to nestle into the large gardens encircling it. It was only two storeys, in white stone, with arched windows and colourful flowerbeds running along the frontage.

They went inside, and Alaina continued to be charmed.

For himself, Rafaello thought it could do with refurbishment, and he said as much.

Alaina cast him a look. 'Your standards are a clearly a good deal higher than mine—it all looks beautiful. And homely.' She glanced around. 'What about the furniture?'

'There's an option to include it, but I assume you would want to start afresh.'

She shook her head. 'It suits the house. And anything new would have to be made Joey-proof! Besides...' she cast him another look '...you can't tell me this house isn't going to cost a great deal of money. You might as well save on furniture.'

Rafaello looked at her. Was she serious?

But she was already wandering off, smoothing the back of a long sofa absently and heading towards the arched French windows that opened onto a terrace beyond. Joey was intently studying a painting on the wall that depicted nymphs lounging around in a classical landscape.

'Those ladies have no clothes on,' he observed. 'Aren't they cold?'

'Fortunately, it's summer time for them,' Rafaello said. 'And in Italy the summers are always hot.'

'So will we go around without clothes in summer?' Joey enquired.

'Not entirely,' Rafaello answered. 'But when we are in our garden we may not want to wear much. Especially when—'

But Joey was running forward excitedly. He'd been leading the way to the French windows, and Rafaello had followed him. Beyond the covered terrace, plentifully arrayed with planters rich with greenery and verdant with bright flowers, azure water sparkled in the sunshine.

'A swimming pool!' he exclaimed ecstatically. He started to jump up and down in enthusiastic excitement.

'I think that seals the deal,' Rafaello murmured.

Alaina gave a laugh. It struck him that it was the first time he had heard her laugh since five years ago…

She was walking forward, coming to Joey, who was still jumping up and down in glee.

'Can Joey swim?' Rafaello asked.

'Yes, but not without water wings yet. We were allowed to use the hotel's indoor pool sometimes. He loved it!'

'Good,' said Rafaello. 'But I think, all the same, it would be prudent to put some fencing around the pool.'

'Yes,' agreed Alaina.

She looked about her.

'This really is a lovely garden! I know the gardens of the other villas we saw were fabulous, but they were very formal. Here, like I said, there's a homely feel. Plus, the pool is close to the terrace, so that makes overseeing Joey easier.' She frowned slightly. 'Does a gardener come with the place? It's going to take a lot of upkeep!'

'As I have said, there will be staff. This particular villa,' he went on, 'comes with a staff cottage, though we can't see it from here.'

Alaina looked at him. 'I think I'd find it easier if the staff weren't in the house itself. That would make me feel a bit…well, awkward. More like a hotel, I suppose. I wonder what the bedrooms are like? Shall we take a look?'

'There are only five,' Rafaello remarked.

'Sounds plenty!' she answered, calling Joey back to check out upstairs.

Upstairs found as much favour as downstairs, and as Joey ran in and out of the bedrooms eagerly, Rafaello turned to Alaina.

'Decision made?' he asked.

She smiled, and it was a warm smile.

'Yes, please,' she answered.

'Good,' he replied. He caught hold of Joey as he careered around. 'Time for lunch, I think, young man.'

Joey looked up at him. 'Are we going to live here? With the swimming pool?'

'Yes,' he said.

'Hurrah!' said Joey.

Rafaello laughed. Joey's delight was infectious.

He felt his mood lift and his eyes met Alaina's. 'You see,' he said softly, 'we can make this work.'

For a moment he held her gaze, not sure what he was seeing in her expression. Then Joey was tugging at his arm.

'You said it was time for lunch,' he reminded him plaintively. 'And my tummy is *very* hungry.'

Alaina stepped forward, taking Joey's other hand. 'Come on, then, let's go and eat. Careful on the stairs, munchkin, no rushing!'

She set off down the wide stone stairs and Rafaello looked after her for a moment. She walked very gracefully...

He felt memory flicker like the replaying of an old film: their brief time in the Caribbean. How long ago it seemed. And yet—

Joey was calling out for him, telling him again that it was lunchtime, and Rafaello followed them downstairs—his son and the mother of his son. The woman who was, against all expectations, his wife.

He wondered what he was feeling about it other than strange. Then he put it out of his mind. It didn't matter what he was feeling about it. He had done what had to be done and that was all there was to it. Now it was just a question of getting on with it.

Alaina took her place at the table, looking about her with pleasure. The three of them were seated outdoors at a pleasant and to her mind very typical Italian trattoria. It was not the restaurant that Rafaello had first chosen in this little town out in the Roman countryside—which, she had seen at a glance, had been far too elegant for Joey.

She'd said as much, pointing across the *piazza* to a much more humble and therefore child-friendly establishment. Besides, it looked more attractive, with its colourful awning, red-checked tablecloths on the pavement tables, cheerful bright red geraniums in big pots around the perimeter. Much more attractive than the pristine white linen tablecloths and the modernistic clipped box hedges and sculpted topiary of the expensive-looking restaurant.

Rafaello had made no demur, but it was clear it would not have been his choice to eat so cheaply. Memory struck her. On the island, as they'd toured around, she'd opted once for eating lunch on a beach, supplied by a ramshackle bar from which vibrant reggae music had been audible. She could remember her own cajoling banter with Rafaello as she'd squeezed his arm encouragingly.

'Come on—it's local—it looks fun!'

She blinked and the memory was gone.

The trattoria's waitress arrived with menus and a beaming smile which became even more beaming when she laid eyes on Joey. She broke into voluble Italian at the sight of him and Alaina heard *'bambino'* several times. She realised that the Italians' love of children was in full flood and Joey, she could see, was basking in it. Even though he could not understand a word, he knew when he was being praised to the skies.

Then the middle-aged waitress—presumably the proprietor's wife, Alaina thought—made a remark that she did get the gist of.

'So like his *papà*!'

She bustled off, leaving the words ringing in Alaina's head. Leaving, too, a difficult thought in its wake. What if Joey *hadn't* been such a dead ringer for Rafaello? What if his looks had taken after hers, instead? Would Rafaello have thought him to be his child? Or assumed Ryan was the dad?

Then I would not be here now, in Italy, at Rafaello's behest, reshaping my entire life...changing everything I thought it would be...

Emotion flushed through her, but she wasn't sure what it was. Regret for the lost life that she had so carefully made for her and Joey? Or unease at the thought that she had kept all knowledge of Joey's existence from Rafaello? Or was it an even more difficult thought?

Her eyes went to him now, as he paid attention to Joey, going through the menu with him, telling him what the dishes on offer were. His manner towards Joey was hard to decipher. But one thing was obvious. It was not...

Not *what*, precisely? How could she describe it? He was attentive, patient, calm—but not...

Not affectionate. Not paternal. Not loving.

Joey might be any little boy...

A pang pierced her, and yet she had no right to feel it. She had been the one to exclude Rafaello from Joey's life. It had been mere chance that had blown that out of water. But all the same, she argued to herself now, staring at her own menu without taking it in, his dispassionate attitude towards Joey only showed her that she had made the right decision five years ago?

He thinks of Joey as a responsibility. So he's stepped up to the mark to take that on board.

He, too, after all, was changing his life for the sake of the little boy. She felt those strange, confusing emotions tangle inside her again, and then, realising that it did no good to dwell on what she could not change, she set them aside. She was going along with what Rafaello had stipulated—bringing Joey out here, legitimising his existence by entering into marriage with his father—and now she had to deal with that as positively as she could. For Joey's sake.

'Joey's decided on *spaghetti napoletana*,' Rafaello announced.

'Excellent.' Alaina smiled. 'Me too.' She set her own menu down.

'That makes three of us.' Rafaello smiled too, but more faintly.

His words echoed in Alaina's head.

Three of us...

But was there really an 'us' at all when it came to the strange unit they made? Outwardly so normal, yet in reality so totally not...?

But that was going to be their future now, wasn't it? Looking like a normal family—*mamma, papà e bambino*.

Her gaze went to Rafaello, who was beckoning the waitress over to give their order. She felt her breath catch. Dear God, five years had only made him even more good-looking! Whatever it was about his looks—and she knew they were not to all female tastes, with the fine-boned, even austere features, their sometimes saturnine cast, and the lidded eyes that were so often veiled—they reached to her own female susceptibilities as no other man's ever had...

She'd known it five years ago, as she'd embarked on that irresistible affair with him. And with a painful swallow she knew it now, too.

What she was going to do about it, she had no idea.

Except resist it.

Five years ago he didn't want me. Now what he wants is Joey.

Her eyes shadowed.

And what do I want?

Well, that was obvious too. She wanted Joey safe, with her, and happy. That was her priority. The only priority she could have...could allow herself.

Nothing else.

And certainly not what, if she were not strong and resolute, she might be weak enough to want.

For that time had gone. Finished five years go. Rafaello had made that very clear.

The move to the villa was accomplished within a week, Rafaello having insisted on immediate occupancy and expedited all the legalities.

Alaina was relieved. She'd spent the week taking Joey out and about, exploring Rome, treating it as a holiday. Rafaello was at his office daily, but returned to dine with her every evening, usually returning after Joey was in bed. Her conversation with him was mostly about what she and Joey had done that day, and practicalities pertaining to the villa and moving in as swiftly as possible. She'd deliberately kept Joey's toys in their bedroom, which had become a playroom as well, so as to minimise the risk to Rafaello's antiques.

Her relief as they set off for the newly acquired villa was palpable. And not just on Joey's account. On her own, as well.

She was getting used to Rafaello's presence in her life. But it was not easy. That sense of unreality that had hit on their wedding day washed over her periodically, and sometimes she awoke in the mornings longing so much to be back home, in her own life, the way she had been living it. But that was impossible now. It had gone.

Now I just have to get on with this life.

Was it any easier for Rafaello? She had made more of a change to her life than he had—except, of course, she had to acknowledge that she wasn't dealing with discovering that she was a parent...

It was hard to tell what he was thinking...feeling. He was unfailingly courteous and accommodating towards her, unfailingly patient and attentive to Joey, and his calm, unruffled demeanour was, she had to acknowledge, making it all that much easier for her. Or at least less difficult...

'You will be glad to know,' he was saying to her now, as they headed out of the city, 'that the married couple who looked after the villa's previous occupants are happy to stay on. I hope they prove satisfactory.'

The greeting that Maria and Giorgio afforded them on their arrival indicated to Alaina at least that they would indeed prove satisfactory. They were middle-aged, with smiling, kindly faces, and Maria's English was perfectly adequate. Giorgio's was enthusiastic, if less fluent, and their faces lit up when Joey descended from the car.

Joey had clearly acquired two more fans, and beamed angelically. Then Giorgio was fetching the luggage and Maria was bustling off, promising lunch *'prontissimo'*.

They ate in the pleasantly appointed dining room, the doors open to the terrace, and Joey made a hearty meal of his pasta, fussed over by Maria, who was still demonstrating her enchantment with him.

Through the open French windows Alaina could see the sun sparkling off the water of the swimming pool—and saw, too, that a metre-high fence with a lockable gate was now encircling the pool area.

'That was swiftly done!' she exclaimed.

'Essential things can always be done swiftly,' Rafaello replied. 'When there is pressing need and the will and the means to do them.'

Her eyes went to him. Thoughts raced in her head.

Like marrying the woman you've discovered has had your child... Then moving them both out to Italy and into a villa that will be their new home...

Well, it was done now. She was married to him and here she and Joey were. At the villa. Their new home. She felt emotion stir somewhere inside her but would not pay it any attention. There was no point in doing so. No point in doing anything other than accepting the situation in which she found herself.

Rafaello was speaking again.

'I'm going to leave you and Joey to settle in,' he was saying, in that cool, imperturbable way of his. 'Let you find your feet—that is the expression, is it not? I'll go back to the apartment, and then later this coming week I have to fly to Geneva for a few days. I hope Maria and

Giorgio will look after you well, but of course you must phone me if there is anything you need me to do.'

She nodded. It was true—it would be easier for her and Joey to settle in here without Rafaello being around. Without him she could relax. Did he see that in her expression now? His gaze was resting on her unreadably, but she felt he could read her all too easily.

He gave his familiar faint smile. 'Take your time, Alaina. It will get easier, I promise you. For both of us. We shall...get used to things.'

She nodded again. 'I know, but—'

She broke off. What was there to say? They would *have* to get used to things, that was all.

She deliberately put a more upbeat expression on her face. 'Thank you for agreeing to this villa, Rafaello. I think it will suit us very well. And Maria and Giorgio too. As you say, given time, we'll...get used to things.'

Her gaze slid away, for all that, moving around the room in this villa that was now going to be her home. Hers and Joey's. The strangeness of it lapped at her, and she heard a low sigh escape her.

Then, giving a little start, she felt Rafaello's hand lightly touch hers as it lay on the table. It was lifted away swiftly, as she heard him speak again.

'We did what we had to do, Alaina—both of us.' He nodded towards Joey, who was busy polishing off his *dulce*—a sweet, nutty cake confection bestowed upon him by Maria. 'For his sake,' he said.

And that, in the end, was what it came down to—what it always came down to.

What else could she do but remember it and accept it?

She blinked, and realised with a disquiet that had nothing to do with this new life being forced upon her, that she could still feel the echo of his brief touch to her hand…

Rafaello's touch…

CHAPTER FIVE

RAFAELLO SLID THE key into his hotel room door and entered with a sense of relief. He'd shower, shave, and dine out. He felt he needed it. His client, objecting to a particularly hefty tax bill, had been difficult and demanding, and clearly displeased with the recommendations Rafaello had made, which did not reduce the amount payable as much as he wanted.

Rafaello's mouth curved cynically. Since he wanted to pay none of it, he was bound to be dissatisfied.

A mood of irritation swept over him. He wanted to be done with this particularly irksome client, however profitable he was to the firm. He wanted, he thought, as he methodically stripped off his jacket and constricting tie, followed by his shirt and the rest of his clothes as he headed for the en suite bathroom, to get back to Rome.

He wanted to see Joey.

And not just Joey.

The realisation came to him as he stepped into the shower and turned the water to max.

I want to see Alaina.

The water, hot and forceful, was sluicing over him powerfully, stinging on his skin. The sensation was physical, potent. Almost…

No!

He reached to snap the temperature down. Stood there, shocked, as colder water poured over him.

But as he started to wash himself, rigorously and swiftly, he was physically aware of his own body in ways he was loath to acknowledge. Yet the knowledge impressed itself upon him all the same.

As he rinsed himself off, cut the water, and seized a towel to snake around his hips, another to pad his torso dry, his thoughts were…difficult. Shaking his wet hair, he stepped up to the sink, reaching for his razor, starting the familiar ritual of a wet shave. As he did so, he stared at his reflection. Scrutinising it as if it were a hostile witness.

He wanted to find out the truth he was concealing.

From himself.

He paused, razor in hand, his gaze boring into his own eyes.

From the very moment his gaze had gone to the little boy at Alaina's desk in the hotel, and realisation had struck him like a tsunami pulverising him, he had gone into a mode of behaviour that was what the situation—an unimagined situation—demanded of him. Of him and of Alaina. Nothing else had been permissible. He had pushed it forward remorselessly, ruthlessly, demolishing everything that might stand in the way of getting to where he now was. Where Alaina was too.

Everything else had been put to one side.

Including the past. His gaze narrowed. The past that had created the very situation he had now dealt with. Was still dealing with.

They had married for the sake of the son they had unintentionally created. That was as far ahead as he had thought—had allowed himself to think. But now they were married. Now Alaina and Joey were safely installed in the villa he had found for them. Now their new lives were underway. And so was his new life.

Alaina, the woman he had romanced all those years ago, was back in his life. Married to him. His entire focus had been on getting to this point. He had barely thought beyond it. But now, deed done, marriage accomplished, he knew with unavoidable clarity that he had to do just that—think beyond simply making Alaina his wife.

They were married, yes. But…

But what kind of marriage are we going to have?

Oh, he had said they would be civil and civilised about it, and that was what they were being. And, yes, he had talked of a vague future when separation might not be out of the question, when Joey was old enough and they might go their separate ways. But till then…?

He reached for his shaving foam, applied it with smooth, methodical strokes, brought the blade of his razor down his cheeks, along the line of his chin. Familiar, routine movements… And all the time his eyes were boring into those in his reflection. Asking a question to which he already knew the answer.

The question about what kind of marriage he and Alaina were going to have.

The answer literally stared him in the face, shaping itself in words that spelt it out with clarity and concision and compelling logic.

I desired her once.

He had desired her from the moment he had seen her, her lovely body displayed to the sun, so long ago on that silver sand beach under the hot Caribbean sun. He had desired her, courted her, seduced her—and she had come with him every step of the way. Her lovemaking had been as ardent as his…her passion, unleashed at his touch, as hot as his.

So why should it not be so again?

Because how else was their marriage going to work?

The logic of his thoughts clicked ineluctably into place, making him accept it as his gaze bored into his reflection in the glass. Adultery was abhorrent, unthinkable—either hers or his. And celibacy…

A glint showed in his dark eyes. Well, he knew himself well enough to know that the prospect of celibacy—indefinite, on-going celibacy, for any length of time—would be…challenging.

But why should he—or she—be contemplating either unpalatable prospect? There was no reason for it. There was proof positive, after all, of just how compatible they were in that respect. And nothing had changed, after all, had it?

Five years on he acknowledged that Alaina's beauty, though matured now, was every bit as breathtaking as it had been when they'd first romanced. He had suppressed his awareness of it because it had been a distraction from his focus on getting his son into his life the way he had. But now—wedding over, their removal to Italy accomplished, her settled at the villa with the son he had claimed—now he could indulge that awareness.

As for Alaina… Well, the same logic drove his thoughts forward. Why should she be immune to the charms that she had once found as irresistible as he had found hers? She, after all, had made it clear at the time that she would have liked their time together to continue.

The glint came into his eyes again. Well, now their

time together *could* continue. With a little encouragement on his part…

Into his head came the words he had said to her.

'*We can make this work.*'

The glint in his eyes intensified and he set aside his razor, its work done, bent to rinse his face and pat it dry. Then he looked once more at his reflection.

They could indeed make this marriage work.

And not just for the sake of their son and the stability of his family life.

We can make it work for us—for Alaina and myself— as well as our son.

He dropped the towel beside the basin, strode out into the bedroom and swiftly dressed again—more casually this time—for dinner at a nearby restaurant.

His mood was better than it had been for quite some time. Tomorrow he'd be heading home. To Joey—and Alaina.

Anticipation filled him.

Alaina stretched languorously. She was face-down on a flat sun lounger, out on the villa's sunlit terrace. This early in the summer it was deliciously warm, but not too hot, and the afternoon sun felt extremely pleasant on her bare back.

Somewhere in the gardens she could hear water sprinkling, and Joey's piping voice every now and then, coupled with Giorgio's deeper one. Birdsong came from the bushes, and the scent of flowers. A little way off she could hear the lap of water in the pool, slapping gently against the filter. Sleep drifted over her and she drowsed lazily in the warmth. It really was gorgeous to be able to sunbathe like this, knowing she had the leisure to do so and that Joey was happy without her attention.

Memory plucked at her. How long ago it was that she had sunbathed on that silver sand beach in the Caribbean…?

She dozed off again, sleepy under the sun.

Why she awoke, she did not know. Footsteps on the paving stones?

She lifted her head, expecting to see Giorgio returning with Joey. It was not.

It was Rafaello.

Looking at her from the shade of the covered terrace, standing in one of the arches, completely still. Just looking at her.

Looking her over.

Past and present rushed together. That was exactly the way he'd looked at her—looked her over—that long-ago afternoon in the Caribbean. In that chance encounter that had led to the present moment…

She felt her cheeks flare, a heat flush through her that had nothing to do with the sun and everything to do with the way his gaze was resting on her. So very, very familiar…

In those few heady weeks that she'd spent with him how often had she seen his gaze on her like that? Countless times! And every time it had melted her, sent a dissolving heat through her, quickened her pulse, licking at her senses.

Faintness washed through her and she dipped her head.

Then she heard: 'Where's Joey?'

Rafaello's voice was sharp, and her head shot up as he strode towards her.

'Joey…?' She said it vaguely, as if the name were unfamiliar to her.

Her eyes were riveted on him. She hadn't seen him for several days and now he was walking towards her, his impeccable business suit moulding his tall frame. She took in the silk of his grey tie, the pristine cuffs. He looked sleek, and expensive, and lethal…

'Where is he?' he demanded again, and his gaze raked the pool, even though the gate was firmly shut.

She pulled herself up, careful to ensure that she took the sarong she was lying on with her as she did, remaining punishingly aware that if she let it slip she'd be naked to the waist, for the strings of her bikini were undone.

'He's with Giorgio,' she retorted, stung at the implicit accusation in Rafaello's question. Deftly, she managed to knot the sarong over her breasts, and got to her feet. 'They're watering the plants in the shade.'

Rafaello frowned.

Alaina went on, with an indulgent smile in her voice. 'Joey,' she informed Rafaello, 'happens to adore watering the garden! And Giorgio has a hose…*much* more fun than a mere watering can.' She gave a fond laugh. 'I can only hope that the plants are getting some of the water at least!'

She saw Rafaello's expression relax. At least as far as Joey's safety was concerned. But then his eyes came back to her, and in them was, once again, the same look as before. She stood for a moment, knowing that the thin material of the sarong was moulding the shape of her breasts, and that her shoulders were completely bare. Her hair, roughly pinned on her head to get it off the back of her neck, threatened to descend at any moment. She felt caught off-guard.

Her colour slightly too high, she made an attempt at nonchalance. 'How did it go in Geneva?'

'Tedious,' he replied. 'I'm glad to be back.' He looked about him, taking in his surroundings, his expression changing. 'This was a good choice of yours...this villa.' His tone was considering—and approving.

Alaina's expression softened too. 'It's lovely, isn't it? Perfect for Joey, too. He's been loving the pool, I promise you. He's really settling in.'

Rafaello nodded. 'Good,' he said. 'And, speaking of the pool, it looks pretty tempting right now, I must say.' He turned away. 'I think I'll join you,' he said, heading back indoors.

As he left, Alaina sat herself back down on the lounger with a plonk. Her heart rate was up—she could tell. And it wasn't just because she'd been startled by Rafaello's appearance. Her cheeks felt heated, and she stared out over the sparkling water in the pool, thoughts churning, willing herself to calm down.

Finding it harder than she thought.

Wishing she didn't. But not wanting to examine why.

Rafaello shrugged off his business clothes, pulled on bathing trunks and a white tee, slipped his feet into pool sandals and headed downstairs, pausing only to put his head around the kitchen door and greet Maria, in the throes of making fresh pasta, and ask for coffee and refreshments to be served on the terrace.

Then he went outside, slipping on a pair of sunglasses against the bright sunshine. Wanting to see Alaina again. Knowing just why.

Restlessness filled him, together with an incongruous sense of purpose. He felt conflicted, and at the same time knew his decision had been made. Knew that he wasn't going to unmake it—nor regret it.

As he stepped out on to the cool, shaded and covered terrace, his eyes went straight to Alaina, now sedately sitting on her lounger, its backrest upright. Her upper body was now in shadow under the parasol she'd pulled over the lounger. Only her bare, honey-coloured legs stretched out into the sun.

His decision was confirmed.

He felt again that instinctive quickening of his body, but repressed it. Now was not the occasion.

She looked up from the magazine she'd apparently been perusing intently. She, too, had donned dark glasses, and she had also retied the strings of her bikini, though her body was still securely veiled by her colourful sarong.

'Oh, there you are. Do come out and enjoy this sun,' she said to him lightly—and self-consciously, he could tell.

She indicated another sun lounger, and he pulled it into the half-shade of the parasol, facing the glittering water of the pool.

'This really is blissful!' she went on, still in that light, self-conscious voice.

'Definitely an improvement on Geneva—it was raining,' Rafaello responded dryly. He opened the book he'd brought out with him, a popular police thriller. 'I've asked Maria for coffee—and something for Joey too, when he's done with soaking the plants.'

'And soaking Giorgio too, I suspect—and himself!' Alaina added with a smile.

She flicked a few pages of her magazine—an Italian homes and gardens one, Rafaello could see.

He indicated it with his hand. 'Any good ideas for the

villa?' he asked casually. 'You must feel entirely free to refurnish and redecorate, you know. It is your home now.'

'It's lovely as it is,' she assured him. 'But maybe I'll get some new cushions and ornaments...things like that. Oh, and some pool toys!'

'We can get them tomorrow,' Rafaello said genially. 'Joey can help choose them.'

'He'll love that!' Alaina laughed.

Maria emerged from the house with a tray of coffee, juice, iced water and some tempting-looking *biscotti*, setting it down and then disappearing again.

Rafaello watched Alaina busy herself pouring for them both. He took the proffered cup, knowing his fingers lightly brushed hers. Knowing that she knew they had...

He sat back, sipping his coffee. He would take this slowly. Not rush things but savour them... As he had before.

The prospect was pleasing.

He took another mouthful of his coffee, relaxing his shoulders back. After all the last few weeks had necessitated, it was time to relax. Relax and...enjoy.

His eyes flickered sideways for a moment. In profile, Alaina was as beautiful as in full face: the delicate line of her cheek, her hair in tendrils around her jaw, her mouth tender and sensuous. All of it as alluring to him now as five years ago.

Every bit as alluring...

Alaina clutched her magazine a tad more tightly than required and knew why. She was punishingly conscious of Rafaello, sitting beside her on the adjacent lounger. Punishingly conscious of how his long, bare, lithely muscled legs were stretched out...how the white tee moulded his lean torso. Conscious, most of all, of how she wanted to twist her head and drink him in.

Memory was crowding her head. Of how they'd sunned themselves on the beach in the Caribbean, heating up only to cool off in the turquoise water, she in her skimpy bikini, he stripped to the waist. Then they'd gone to his room, in the cool of the air-con, and he'd slid his arms around her, drawn her down onto the bed, removing the frail barrier of her bikini to have her naked in his arms, to make love to her...

She tried to push the memory out, but it was reluctant to go. She felt colour flush her cheeks, and hoped Rafaello was not looking at her. Let alone realising why she blushed.

She felt danger flicker inside her. In the weeks since Rafaello had walked back into her life with such devastating consequences she'd done her best not to let herself remember, not to let herself acknowledge that whatever it was he possessed that had been so lethal to her, he still had it. She had let herself think no further than what he was demanding of her—that she marry him, that she uproot herself, settle in Italy, make her home here with Joey.

And with him.

And now it was done. She was here. Married. Settled in their new home.

And what happens now? Between Rafaello and me?

The question floated inchoate, barely formed. But she didn't want to give it shape or substance. Didn't want it there at all. She had thought no further than getting to this point because she had had no alternative but to do so. But now...

'Mummee!'

The patter of Joey's feet was a welcome interruption

to thoughts she did not want to have…questions she did not want to ask. He came running up to her, his tee shirt, as she'd predicted, soaking wet.

'We've been watering—Giorgio and me! He let me have the hose! We got wet!'

'So you did, munchkin,' she agreed.

'Very wet,' Rafaello confirmed beside her.

Joey noticed his presence and ran around the lounger to him. 'Papà!' He tugged at Rafaello's arm. 'Come swimming! Come swimming!' he begged excitedly.

Rafaello swung his legs round, getting to his feet. 'You'll need your water wings,' he reminded Joey.

Alaina handed Joey some diluted juice to gulp down, with a *biscotti* to munch on, while she peeled off the soaking tee shirt and stripped off his shorts—almost as wet—getting his wriggling body into swimming trunks, then sliding the inflated armbands on as he jumped from one foot to the other impatiently.

Then Rafaello was taking his hand, walking to the pool with him, unlocking the gate.

'Jump in! Jump in!' Joey cried excitedly, and proceeded to do just that.

Alaina watched Rafaello enter the water more sedately as Joey batted around in his armbands. She watched them, emotion moving within her.

Father and son…

But what kind of father would Rafaello make? He talked of responsibilities, and he was unfailingly patient with Joey, but what else?

It will come in time, won't it? That bond must surely form?

Yet it did not always.

A shiver went through her. Had she been a boy, perhaps her father would have taken more notice of her. Or had she developed the same interests he had when she'd reached her teenage years. But that had never happened. It was her mother she had been close to—the mother who had warned her, from her own bitter experience, to be careful where she gave her heart. Never, never to give it to a man who could not return her love…

A shadow seemed to fall over her and she heard again in her head her mother's sad warning.

Her gaze, of its own volition, went to the two figures in the pool. Her son, so eager and excited, and the man who had fathered him. The man to whom she had once given herself in passion and desire, coming so close to wanting more than he could offer her, to wanting what she had come so close to offering him…

And once again danger flickered all around her. Impossible to dispel.

CHAPTER SIX

'MARIA, THANK YOU. This all looks splendid. We'll serve ourselves.' Rafaello gave a cool, but appreciative smile to the housekeeper.

She bustled out, having set the plentiful array of dishes on the table for them to help themselves.

Rafaello reached for the wine he'd selected. He'd had a delivery from the wine merchant he patronised, and now he poured carefully for Alaina and himself. She was sitting opposite him, and his eyes rested on her with appreciation.

She'd come down from checking on Joey in bed, and Rafaello's glance had immediately gone to her. Though not formally dressed—for that was not necessary here at the villa—she wore a calf-length shift dress in warm amber tones, with a light lacy cardigan. It flattered her slender figure. Her hair was in a casually upswept style that was equally flattering to her bone structure. She had not put on make-up…but that hardly mattered. Her eyes, wide-set and long-lashed, barely needed enhancing, and nor did the tender curve of her mouth. In the soft light from the wall lamps she looked effortlessly lovely.

'So,' he announced, lifting his wine glass, 'our first weekend here. *Saluti.*'

He tilted his glass and took a considering mouthful before giving the wine his approval. Then he set his glass back on the table, lifting the lids of the various serving bowls placed on chafing dishes to keep them warm. Maria had prepared a rich beef ragout, with slices of grilled polenta and assorted steamed vegetables.

He gave a generous helping to Alaina, and then to himself. 'Well, I see we won't starve with Maria in charge of the kitchen!' he remarked drily.

Alaina gave a little laugh. 'No, indeed. She's feeding Joey up on pasta and pastries very nicely—though I make sure he's eating lots of salad and fruit as well,' she added. 'He's taken to Italian cooking like a natural!'

Rafaello's eyes glinted as he made a start on the delicious ragout. 'Well, he is half-Italian. And now,' he said pointedly, 'he can give free rein to that side of his heritage.'

He saw colour stain her cheekbones as she picked up her fork.

'He's adapting well,' was all she said in reply.

'And you?'

Her eyes met his across the table. 'I'm doing my best,' she said.

Was there defensiveness in her tone of voice? There was no need for it.

'I appreciate, Alaina, what you've done.'

Something changed in her expression and her eyes dropped away. She gave a little shrug, barely a gesture at all.

In a deliberately lighter tone, he went on. 'How have you busied yourself this week?'

She took the cue and answered in a similarly light tone. 'We've unpacked, and Joey's chosen his bedroom—that's his playroom too, so his toys shouldn't spread too widely! We've done a lot of pool time—Joey's favourite! And Giorgio very kindly drove us into the nearby town so we could explore and stock up on some bits and pieces.'

'I must ensure you have a suitable car for yourself and Joey,' Rafaello remarked. 'Can you face driving out here?'

'I must,' she answered. 'I don't want to rely on Giorgio—or you—the whole time. But maybe I should take a few lessons—learn how to drive on the wrong side of the road!' she added humorously.

She paused, taking another sip from her wine, then went on.

'I'm wondering whether it would be good to find some kind of nursery for Joey. Oh, not a full-time nursery, obviously, but maybe a few mornings a week…to help him socialise, and most of all to help him learn Italian. He's picking up some from Maria and Giorgio—and you, of course,' she acknowledged. 'He's made a start, but it's best he becomes as fluent as possible, as swiftly as possible.'

'I agree,' Rafaello answered. He looked across at her. 'And what about you? Do you want an Italian tutor?'

She made a face. 'That sounds very formal. I brought a couple of grammar books out with me from the UK. I bought them when…when I knew I was going to have to come out here,' she said, and he could hear the awkwardness in her voice. 'And there's the Internet too, of course— loads of how to learn Italian podcasts!'

'Well, if you want one-on-one tuition, just say. Of course,' he added, his voice smooth, 'I can always provide that myself.'

He let his gaze rest on her for a moment. She'd flushed a little, and he liked the effect it had on her. Liked it considerably…

His mood mellowed even more.

'I seem to remember,' he said musingly, his gaze still on her, 'that you showed an aptitude for acquiring a... specialised vocabulary when we first knew each other...'

The flush increased, and he knew exactly why.

Memory washed within him of how she had lain in his embrace, after lovemaking, her mouth gliding over his anatomy, asking him the Italian for each place where her lips were languorously exploring...

She bent her head, busying herself with the business of doing justice to Maria's cooking. He knew why. He let her be. To pursue the subject would be crass.

Instead, he took another mouthful of wine and made some remark about it, which she picked up on, asking him a question about what kind of wine it was. He told her, and let the subject be a suitable topic for anodyne discourse. He saw her heightened colour subside, and she visibly relaxed once more.

'Well, as you can tell, I know nothing about wine,' she said lightly. 'But this...' she indicated her glass '...is certainly very good.'

'Thank you,' he murmured, half amused. 'I shall look forward to building a cellar here, I think. I must explore the kitchen and decide the best position for installing it.'

'Doesn't it have to be a hole in the ground?' she asked, surprised.

'Not at all. These days climate-controlled cabinets are superior in many ways. Adjusting them minutely for temperature and humidity and so forth is a fine art.'

'I'm sure you'll have fun with it,' she answered, her voice dry. But he heard amused indulgence in her tone as well.

'What is that phrase in English?' he queried lightly. 'Boys' toys? Is that it?'

She gave a laugh. 'Spot on,' she agreed.

He was glad of the light mood, and of the mild, but significant rapport it betokened. He felt his good mood improve even more and reached again for his own wine glass, relaxing back in his comfortable dining chair.

Things were coming along nicely…

Alaina pushed her now-empty dessert bowl away from her with a little sigh. Maria had concocted a delicious *semifreddo* and Alaina had been unable to resist it. She sat back, replete but relaxed. Surprisingly relaxed…

There had been a couple of awkward moments during the meal, but they had passed and conversation had become more general…easier. Yet for all that those moments had been disquieting. Oh, not when Rafaello had pointedly reminded her that Joey was half-Italian, but when he'd reminded her of other things.

Lying in his arms…asking him what the Italian word was for the place where I was kissing him…

She pulled her mind away—but not sufficiently to blank all those memories…memories only too easily aroused simply by dining with him here, by the French windows open to the terrace, with the sound of cicadas beyond, the mild warmth of the air, the perfume from the night-scented flowers in the gardens.

All of it was weaving memories into her head.

Rafaello taking her to dinner at a seductively situated restaurant…dining out on a terrace overlooking a moonlit beach below. The murmur of waves, the caressing warmth of the evening, the candle glowing in its glass holder as he poured wine for her, refilled her glass… His lambent gaze telling her how very appealing she was to him and her own gaze resting on him in return, reciprocating the message.

He'd lifted his glass to her, and she hers to him, and his hand had reached for hers across the table, softly letting his long, sensitive fingers play on the delicate contours of her exposed wrist—a prelude, tantalising and arousing, of what the rest of the night would bring...of the sensual pleasures that awaited her in the midnight hours...

She could feel the allure of those memories—and knew the danger they held. A danger she must resist, even as she must resist the memories. They had no place in her life now.

She gave her head a little shake, as if to dispel them. 'I ought to check on Joey,' she announced.

'No need,' came the reply. 'We'll hear him on the monitor if he wakes.'

She watched Rafaello get calmly to his feet and cross to the sideboard where Maria had deposited the coffee tray when she'd cleared the table and left their dessert and *formaggio*.

'Let's have coffee on the terrace—it's warm enough, I think,' Rafaello was saying now.

He picked up the tray, gestured towards the French windows for her to go through first. She did so, stepping out on to the terrace.

'The moon has risen,' Rafaello remarked, following her out.

He placed the coffee tray on the low table in front of a rattan couch set back under the arched perimeter of the terrace, sitting himself down beside her, pouring her coffee and his own, handing it to her.

She took it, but knew she was too conscious of Rafaello's presence beside her...the faint, familiar catch of his aftershave, the closeness of his long, lean body that once, so long ago she had known intimately…

She was too conscious of the silvered moon riding high in the heavens, of the shimmering iridescence of the pool water, lit from underneath, the murmurous chorus of cicadas all around, the warmth of the early summer evening lapping at her. All conspired to evoke memory within her. Memory she should not allow.

It came all the same.

She and Rafaello, sitting out on the balcony of his room at the Falcone, with the moon glancing over the Caribbean, the tree frogs audible in the velvet night. Rafaello loosely holding her hand in his, then raising it to his lips, caressing it lightly with the softest silken touch and drawing her to her feet. Rafaello taking her inside, into the air-conditioned cool, where the sensual burn of their passion would give all the heat they needed.

And she going with him so willingly, heat building up in her, pulse quickening… The arousal that had teased her all evening being finally, gloriously, blissfully, meltingly sated as she feasted on him and he on her… Until dawn broke from the east and slumber finally took their spent, exhausted bodies…

She dipped her head, closed her eyes, wanting only to banish the memory. And yet—

She felt the slightest, lightest touch at the nape of her bowed neck. For a second—less than a second—she was sure she felt it. The merest drift of the tips of his fingers, resting on the delicate exposed arc of her neck, playing in the stray fronds of her upswept hair.

A wave of weakness went through her. The sensation was so slight—and yet it was slaying her…

She heard her name spoken. Felt her coffee cup being

removed from her suddenly nerveless grip. Still with her neck bowed forward, her eyes still closed, she felt the fingers of Rafaello's other hand shape her jaw, her cheek, turn her head towards him.

Her eyes opened, wide and fearful. This must not be— she must not let this happen. Must *not*.

But he was leaning towards her, his face half shadowed. The skilled, sensual mouth she had once known so well, whose power to evoke sensations in her that must melt her, beguile her, was reaching for hers now…impossible to prevent.

Impossible to *want* to prevent.

He said her name again, soft and low, and then his mouth was cool on hers. Light, undemanding, and yet with a certainty that told her she must resist.

But how? How to resist what he was drawing from her? How to stop the silken sensation of his mouth moving on hers slowly, lightly, leisurely? How to stop the feathering of his fingers at the nape of her neck? Her head was rising now, as his mouth moved on hers and his hand shaped her cheek. How to stop her own hand lifting with a will of its own to press against the lean, hard wall of his chest, so close, so tantalising, temptingly close to her now?

She let her eyes flutter shut, helpless to do anything but sink into the sensations playing at her mouth, her nape, at the lobe of her ear, into the sensual pressure he brought to bear.

His kiss started to deepen. Her hand against his chest splayed out, her mouth started to move against his, desire quickened within her…

With a cry, she pulled away. Urgently—fearfully.

She forced herself to her feet, stepped back…away.

'Rafaello, no—*no*!'

He was untroubled by her refusal. He sat back, one arm stretched out along the back of the rattan seat, looking up at her. His face was still in the *chiaroscuro* of the moonlight, his body lean and long, as he casually hooked one leg over his knee in a relaxed gesture.

'Why?' he asked.

His question was interested, no more than that, as his half-shadowed gaze rested on her.

'Because…' she said.

Her voice was tight. Her whole body was tight. Yet her heart was pounding—she could feel it. Could feel the adrenaline rush that had come. Whether from his kiss— or her fear of it—or both.

She saw his eyebrows rise. 'Because…?' he prompted.

She clenched her hands at her sides, still feeling her heart pound. Still feeling how dangerously close she had come to that doomed, destructive edge she must never approach.

'Because I don't want to go back into the past!'

He gave that faint, familiar smile, effortlessly demolishing her desperate defence.

'But this is not the past, Alaina. This is the present. And we can acknowledge, with honesty and clarity, that what once drew us together is doing so again.'

He stood up, stepping towards her as he spoke, lifting one hand, letting one finger drift lightly down her cheek.

'You are more beautiful now than ever,' he said, and his voice was low, husky, and did things to her she must not allow. 'So…' He paused, and his eyes, lidded and dark…so dark…held hers. 'Why should we not once more indulge in each other?' His grew even more husky. 'I promise we would find much pleasure for us both…'

She gazed up at him, helpless, in thrall to that darkly

lidded gaze, that low, husky voice. She felt her body sway, weakness drumming though her. Weakness and wanting…

How easy it would be—how very, *very* easy—to let her hands lift to his chest, to feel that hard, familiar wall beneath her fingers, to lift her mouth to his, feel his lips descend on hers to taste and take…

To fall into his arms…his bed…

As she had before.

She felt herself take an unsteady, jerking step back.

'I… I must check on Joey!'

The words were broken, her breath ragged, her pupils dilated.

She turned and fled.

Rafaello watched her go, his expression unreadable. Then, after leaving her sufficient time, he strolled back into the dining room and crossed to the sideboard where he would find the very good single malt his wine merchant had also delivered.

He poured himself a glass, hearing Alaina's hurried footsteps on the stairs. He knew just why she was hurrying—and it was not to check on Joey.

A smile played about his mouth as he strolled back out on to the terrace and lowered himself down on to the rattan couch, stretching out his legs in a leisurely fashion, crossing them at his ankles while he sampled the single malt, his gaze resting on the iridescent water in the pool beyond, hearing the gentle slap of the water interspersed with the night music of the cicadas.

He would not rush her. He would take his time, and she could take hers too. Take all the time needed for her to accept what he had said to her. That there was no reason—

none at all—for them to deny what still ran between them. Five years ago he had had his life to return to—the familiar life he had made for himself, comfortable and well chosen. But that life was gone now—for the foreseeable future. So what reason was there not to make the most of what this new life offered?

When both of them so clearly desired it…

Because what he had revealed to her had been just that—desire. What had been between them five years ago was still there, needing only a touch, a caress, a kiss, to be reawakened…

He relaxed back against the padding of the couch, taking another indulgent mouthful of his whisky, feeling the mature, fine and fiery heat ease down his throat. He savoured it—just as soon he would be savouring all that his reawakened desire for the woman who was now joined to him in marriage would bring him.

It was a marriage he had never planned to make, but now that he had made it, it would bring pleasures of its own to both of them. His dark, lidded eyes glinted in the moonlight, filling with anticipation.

Alaina sat beside Joey as he lay asleep in his bed. Her hand was resting lightly on his head, as if in blessing. Love poured from her, overwhelming and all-consuming. How she loved him! He was everything to her—everything! A precious, wonderful gift she had never looked for, never asked for, and yet his coming had transformed her. She would do anything for him—anything!

And she already had, hadn't she? She'd uprooted her life, turned it upside down, moved to a new country. Rafaello had said that this very evening. Rafaello…the man she had married to protect Joey. Oh, she had done so much for Joey, and she would do more for him! Anything…

Her face shadowed and she lifted her hand away.

But what Rafaello was asking of her now—could she do that?

She got to her feet, looking around blindly for a moment. Feelings washed around inside her like water let out from behind a sluice gate. A sluice gate that had remained shut for five long years.

Her eyes were blind in the dim light of Joey's bedroom, with only the soft, shaded glow of the nightlight plugged into the wall socket at floor level lifting the dark. Joey's breathing was silent, and the room was still…quite still. The only sound was the beating of her heart. That uncertain, troubled beating. She stood there, with questions in her head she could not answer. Did not want to answer.

Then, as if on a sudden impulse, she stooped to drop a feathered kiss on Joey's brow and left the room.

Still she heard no answer to her troubling thoughts, her unanswerable questions.

CHAPTER SEVEN

RAFAELLO STOOD IN front of the cheval glass in his bedroom, tying his black tie with deft, economic movements. Alaina had arrived here at the apartment after lunch, and he had cut his working day short. Joey was safely at the villa, being looked after by Maria and Giorgio.

Tonight he was taking Alaina out with him for the very first time. She had been reluctant at first, but he had simply said, 'Alaina, I won't hide you away at the villa! There is a certain amount of socialising that I do, and it is fitting that you are at my side. Besides...' he had lidded his eyes '...don't you think I want to show you off?'

He'd said it lightly, and lightly was the way he'd been behaving towards her since she had run from him after he'd kissed her that evening after dinner, on the moonlit terrace two weekends ago. He had known he would not... *must* not...rush her...must give her time to accept what he had already accepted.

We can have again what we had before.

It was as simple as that—to him. But if she needed more time...well, she could have it.

The day after she'd run from him he'd made sure to make no reference to it...to behave as they had come to behave with each other—civilly, calmly, congenially, even. They'd spent an easy day enjoyably, taking Joey to buy a selection—a large one!—of pool toys, and then they had gone to have lunch at the same little trattoria Alaina had chosen when they were house-hunting. Then they'd gone back to the villa, and Joey had blissfully tried out all the pool toys.

That evening the weather had been warm enough for Rafaello to suggest a barbecue, and Joey's bliss had gone overboard. By the time he'd consumed the very last burger, the very last grilled banana with ice cream, he'd been all but asleep. Rafaello had carried him upstairs, feeling strange, for it had been unfamiliar, how good it had felt to do so.

Downstairs once more, he had whiled away an hour with Alaina watching a popular crime drama on TV, set in Sicily, and handily provided with subtitles in English for her. It had been an easy, enjoyable evening, without him making any indication or giving her any reminder of what had passed the previous evening.

Sunday morning had seen Joey and himself spending most of their time in the pool again, and then, following a leisurely salad lunch, eaten *al fresco*, he had taken his leave and returned to Rome, ready for the working week.

The next weekend had followed a similar pattern, but he'd also driven Alaina and Joey out into the depths of Lazio, to visit a lakeside resort, where they'd gone out in a boat—much to Joey's delight—and then visited a nearby petting zoo, to Joey's even greater delight.

After two such child-centred weekends, though, Rafaello acknowledged that he was looking forward to something more sophisticated this evening.

He felt that glint come into his eyes as he finished tying

his bow tie. He was to have Alaina to himself. Anticipation filled him.

On her arrival at the apartment that afternoon Rafaello had whisked her off again, heading for the Via Condotti, filled with high fashion boutiques.

'You'll need a gown for tonight,' he'd told her. 'It's quite a formal occasion.'

She'd made her choice and now he wanted to see her in it.

He reached for the slim black case on top of the antique tallboy, sliding it into the pocket of his jacket, and strolled from the room, heading for the *saloni* to await Alaina.

She was already there.

He stopped short.

Never had he seen her more beautiful—not even in the Caribbean all those years ago.

Her full-length gown was a delicate pale blue plissé silk that cupped her breasts and fell in graceful folds to her ankles. Her shoulders were bare, only a diaphanous stole, subtly interwoven with silver thread, covering them lightly. A narrow silver belt circled her slender waist. Her hair was styled high in a top knot, from which delicate strands framed her face.

And her face…

His connoisseur's scrutiny told him everything he needed to know. Full *maquillage*, but applied with a lightness of touch that only enhanced the natural sculpture of her cheekbones, the depth of her luminous eyes, lengthening her lashes and widening her gaze, just as the pastel lipstick enhanced the lovely curve of her mouth.

He let his gaze explore her beauty in a leisurely fashion, knew there was appreciation and approval in his regard of her. With part of his awareness he saw that colour was flaring slightly but significantly across her cheekbones. He was glad of it. It was what he wanted to see. He wanted her to know just how beautiful he thought her.

A sentiment he echoed now in words.

'You look,' he said, strolling towards her now, 'quite breathtaking.'

He felt a smile tug at his mouth. Part warm and genuine…part something else. And a touch—just a touch—saturnine.

'You require only one further adornment,' he said.

He withdrew the jewellery case from his pocket, flicked open the satin top. A river of diamonds lay within. He heard her breath catch as he lifted out the necklace, came near to her to drape it around her throat.

'Rafaello—I couldn't possibly—'

He fastened the safety catch and lightly turned her around, so that he could see the effect of the necklace.

'Exquisite,' he said. 'And quite perfect for you.'

He stood a moment longer, surveying her, admiration open in his eyes. In the Caribbean, when they'd gone out in the evenings, she'd dressed with flair and allure, her chosen colours vibrant to match the climate—vivid vermilions and sunshine-yellows and sea-green blues—but here, for the formal affair ahead of them, her air of mature sophistication, of Italian couture, was exactly appropriate.

'Shall we go?' he murmured, and ushered her forward.

Out on the pavement his car was waiting for them. He opened the rear door for her, letting the driver stay at the wheel.

As she settled herself into the capacious leather seat, drawing the seat belt across her, she spoke.

'Tell me more about this evening, so I'm prepped for it,' she said.

She was speaking in a tone that told him she was putting aside the compliments he'd paid her…the way his gaze had openly admired her.

Rafaello fastened his own seat belt, taking his cue from her. 'Well, as you know, it's the annual gathering for one of the law societies I belong to. A dinner dance, I think is the English expression. I know many who will be there, and networking is always useful. There will also be friends to introduce you to.'

He paused for a moment as the car moved off.

'It's part of the life I lead, Alaina. I hope you will accept it as such.'

She gave a faint, flickering smile by way of an answer. But nothing more.

Rafaello sat back.

He glanced at her momentarily now, her head averted from him as she looked out of the window at the passing streets of Rome, and felt his breath catch yet again at just how breathtakingly lovely she looked in her evening splendour. The evening would bring what it would bring, but he knew with certainty that the very least of it was the dinner dance ahead of them.

That was only the start of what he was looking forward to…

Alaina stepped carefully out of the car, walking beside Rafaello into the lobby of the Viscari Roma, where tonight's function was to be held. She was burningly conscious of her high heels, her fabulous, terrifyingly expensive gown, and the diamonds around her throat. And conscious, most of all, of the man at her side.

She glanced about her. Knowing her heart rate was

elevated not by the prospect of the evening ahead, but of spending it with Rafaello.

That was the challenge.

Since the night he had kissed her out on the villa's terrace in the moonlight, and she had fled from him…fled from herself, he had, to her abject relief, reverted to the way she had got used to him being since he had turned her life upside down with cool, casual ease. His focus had been on Joey, and that was what she could cope with.

But now…tonight…

She was on show. She knew that. Knew that she was there to be Signora Ranieri, the wife of a prominent lawyer, a member of Rome's high society, or whatever it was called out here, and she did not want to make mistakes.

She looked the part, at least, in a gown that had come with an eyewatering price tag and a necklace of diamonds whose value she dared not even think about.

He ushered her up the grand flight of stairs to the floor where the hotel's banqueting suite was. Like the Falcone, out in the Caribbean, the Viscari was head and shoulders above the hotel chain she'd worked at in England, but she would not be cowed by it. OK, so she was here to be Signora Ranieri, and that was what she would be.

Her chin lifted, and she glided forward, getting used to the extra elevation of her heels.

Guests were mingling in the bar area, and Rafaello was drawing her forward. She put a faint smile on her face, conscious that she was getting some curious looks directed her way, which were soon explained when he introduced her—to exclamations of open surprise.

'Alaina and I go back some way,' Rafaello said in his smooth, urbane way, offering no more than that.

Most of the conversation was in Italian, however, and

all that was required of her was to smile and take little sips from her glass of champagne. Soon they were taking their places at their table, and Alaina felt herself relax more. There were only three other couples there, and they all clearly knew each other well enough to be convivial.

The dinner started to be served, and as the dishes went round and the conversation swapped back and forth from Italian to English, divvied up between the guests around the table, Alaina found her nerves subsiding. Everyone was good company, and even if the conversation turned to the law from time to time it was sufficiently general. She was asked polite questions about the part of England she came from, and how she liked living in Italy, and that led to Rafaello mentioning that he'd taken a villa outside of the city.

'It's more suitable for our little boy,' he announced.

He'd said it in English, and Alaina realised, with a tremor, that he'd intended her to understand the announcement he was making. And the fact that he said it so coolly told her he wanted her to do likewise.

'He adores the pool there!' she said, and smiled.

To their credit, no one probed further, and Joey's unexpected existence seemed to have been tacitly accepted.

'How old is he?' one of the women asked.

'Four—and a handful!' Alaina smiled again.

'Oh, ours is five—and even more of a handful, I promise!' The woman laughed.

'Wait till they hit their teens,' another man warned humorously.

The conversation turned to children, and Alaina relaxed. The announcement had been made, absorbed and accepted. Whatever discussion there might be about why Rafaello Ranieri had turned up with a brand-new wife and a brand-new four-year-old son, out of the blue, it could take place later, Alaina decided.

The woman with the five-year-old leant towards her. 'Maybe we should arrange…what is that English term?… some play dates?'

'Oh, that would be lovely—thank you!' Alaina responded genuinely.

She liked the other woman's easy-going air. Her husband was genial too, and was currently chatting to Rafaello—something about some new legislation going through Parliament, Alaina thought.

By the time the lengthy dinner had finished Alaina was feeling decidedly more at ease. Liqueurs and coffee and petits-fours were circulating, the master of ceremonies was announcing the guest speaker, to polite applause, and Alaina settled back with a glass of orange-scented liqueur and a cup of rich coffee, prepared to be bored by a speech on a subject she knew nothing about in a language she did not understand.

Rafaello leant towards her. 'It won't last too long,' he murmured. 'Then the dancing will start.' He paused. 'You're doing splendidly—thank you.'

Alaina gave a flickering smile, lifting her liqueur glass and taking a sip of the fiery but fragrant liquid. Rafaello's breath had been warm on her throat, the hint of his aftershave potent, the heat of his body close. She'd been very cautious in what she'd drunk all evening, but the modest amount of wine had entered her system, she knew. Or something had…

Rafaello sat back, paying dutiful attention to whatever it was the guest speaker was saying. Her gaze rested on his profile and she felt that 'something' reach inside her again. That slight faintness catching at her. Oh, but she could just gaze and gaze at him! She really could just drink him in...

The way I did when we were together. Just sinking my chin into my hands to gaze and gaze. And he would see me gazing and sometimes laugh, sometimes smile, and sometimes... Sometimes he'd lean casually forward across the dinner table and taste my mouth with his, knowing there was only one way the evening would end—impatient for it, yet savouring the journey too. Toying with each her so as to enhance the consummation when it came...

A silent sigh of longing went through her. How much she had wanted him—desired him—yearned for him... How she had counted the hours till she could go off duty... How she'd badgered her boss to get days off ahead of schedule so she could take off with him...climb into the Jeep he'd hired, or the motorboat he'd commandeered, and head off across the island or along the coastline to find other bays and beaches...

She had been in a state of bliss.

Until the end of the affair came and he put her aside—no longer desired, no longer wanted.

Holiday over...time together over.

He had told her, without intentional cruelty, that theirs had been an interlude of the greatest pleasure—but it had now come to an end.

'You have your life, and I have mine,' he'd said, a faint smile on his face.

And she had felt him withdrawing from her...closing her out. Detaching her from his life. Telling her with his body language and that faint smile and his cool voice that this was something she must accept.

And I did. Because what else could I do except be grateful that it was only the edge of the precipice that

I had come to—not the fatal falling over that I might so easily have done had we had longer together...

She heard again, now, the mantra she'd adopted, telling herself, night after night, in the aftermath of his departure, *You got out in time—just in time.*

The way her mother had not...

Applause roused her, and with a start she realised that the speeches were over and an air of relaxation was settling over the room as people got to their feet and started to mingle. At the far end there was a dance floor, and music came from a band that had materialised, striking up old-fashioned melodies from the inter-war years.

'Shall we?'

Rafaello was murmuring his invitation, accompanying it with a smile. Others at the table were getting to their feet too, and Alaina had no option but to do likewise. Otherwise she would be left alone with Rafaello, and that would probably be worse. Besides, she was here to perform her role as Signora Ranieri and this was simply part of it.

He took her hand, drawing her to her feet, ushering her past the tables towards the dance floor. Then he took her into his arms...

Rafaello felt her body tremble—a fine vibration going through her that transmitted itself to him, telling him just how she was responding to being in his arms like this. It was exactly the response he wanted. But he kept his hold on her light, all the same, not drawing her closer to him, letting her get used to the touch of his hand at her waist, guiding her around the dance floor to the gentle age-old melody.

He could tell how self-conscious she was—saw the faintest stain of colour on her cheek, her face turned away from him, her hand touching his shoulder as lightly as she could. He felt…heard…,the swish of her silk skirts, caught the delicate fragrance of her perfume.

He made no attempt to speak to her, wanting her simply to get used to the sensation of dancing with him. Then, as the music stopped and they halted with the other dancers, he smiled down at her.

'That wasn't too bad, was it?' he said.

'I haven't danced in a long time,' she said, swallowing.

She slipped her hand from his, dropping her hand from his shoulder. Taking her cue, he let go of her waist and walked with her back to their table. Another couple joined them—Gina and Pietro Fratelli, with whom Alaina had discussed play dates earlier. Rafaello had no objection—he liked he couple—and if Alaina palled up with Gina, and Joey and their little boy got on…well, that was all to the good.

He chatted to Pietro, a senior lawyer in one of the government departments, letting Alaina talk small children with Gina. Then another couple returned to the table, and the man gallantly asked Alaina to dance. Rafaello promptly asked his wife in return, and the four of them made their way out on to the dance floor again.

Rafaello soon had another chance to dance with Alaina himself, and this time he felt she was less tense, more relaxed, more accepting of their contact. He made no reference to it, only made small talk to her as they danced, though he was never not conscious of her body so close to his…

The evening wound down and people started to take their leave. Soon he and Alaina were among them, heading downstairs, out to their waiting car, then being driven back to his apartment.

As they settled into the car and it moved off, he turned towards her. 'Survived the ordeal?' he quizzed with a half-smile.

'I enjoyed it,' she replied. 'And I'm glad to have met Gina. I think her little boy and Joey could have fun play dates, and it's just what Joey needs. We're going to fix something for next week—we've exchanged phone numbers. She said she doesn't live far away.'

'No, not that far,' Rafaello agreed. 'And, yes, the Fratellis are a nice couple.'

They chatted a little more about the evening as a whole, and then they had arrived at the apartment. He helped Alaina out, feeling once again her hand trembling very slightly as she let him draw her up. She had become self-conscious again—he could tell.

Inside, he turned to her.

'A nightcap to round off the evening?' he suggested.

He kept it light. No pressure—that would not help his cause.

He saw uncertainty flicker in her face. He thought she was about to agree, but then, with a shake of her head, she demurred.

'It's been a long evening. I think I'll just head straight for bed. Thank you for tonight, Rafaello—it was...well, nicer than I thought it might be.'

He gave a low laugh. 'We'll build on it from there,' he said.

He watched her make her way to her bedroom, swaying elegantly on her high heels, the drape of her skirts swishing gracefully, her head poised, as beautiful from this perspective as from the front. A stab of regret went through him. Should he have tried harder to get her to defer retiring? But he was trying to pace it carefully—a little delay would cost nothing.

As her bedroom door shut he heard her murmur a low 'Goodnight', which he echoed absently and headed for his own bedroom. It adjoined hers and had a communicating door—the staff would think it strange otherwise, and he had no wish to cause gossip of any kind. But the communicating door itself was locked from her side, not his...

He let himself into his bedroom, closed the door quietly behind him. Started to pull loose his bow tie.

He was very conscious, glancing at the communicating door between their bedrooms, of Alaina just beyond...

CHAPTER EIGHT

ALAINA SET DOWN her evening bag on the dressing table, easing her feet out of her high-heeled shoes, feeling relief when her feet were flat again. She flexed her toes. She had implied to Rafaello that she was tired, but she wasn't. She was restless. Her heart rate was elevated. She wanted to feel sleepy, but she didn't—and she knew why.

It had been dancing with Rafaello that had done the damage. Oh, she'd covered it as well as she could, and she'd only danced twice with him anyway, but once was all it had taken.

All it had taken to let memory come rushing back in, to breach her careful defences against him, to make her shamelessly, disastrously, want to hold him closer to her in their dancing embrace, to wind her arms around his neck, lean against him, feel his strength, his masculinity, let desire build, arousal quicken…

She gave a half-smothered cry now, turning away sharply. But that meant she now had a full view of herself in the long mirror inset into the wardrobe. She gazed, wide-eyed at her reflection. Her gown was truly beautiful, graceful and flattering as only a couture gown could be.

For a helpless moment she just went on gazing at herself. Then restlessly she turned away. No point standing there admiring herself! Her hands went to her spine, reaching for the zip, pulling it sharply down, peeling the gown from her. She draped it over the back of a velvet armchair—she'd hang it up in the morning. Just as swiftly she stripped off her underwear, determinedly looking nowhere near her reflection, and grabbed her dressing gown to cover herself. The silky material was cool on her skin, and she was glad.

Then she unpinned her hair, shaking it down. With a start, she realised she was still wearing the diamond necklace Rafaello had adorned her with that evening. Her hands went to her nape, fiddling with the clasp. She started to frown—the safety chain was on, and she couldn't get any purchase on it somehow…it was too intricate.

Several attempts later she gave up the battle. Her face set. She was either going to have to sleep in the damn thing or…

Without conscious volition, and without thinking about it—because to do that would have been to stop her in her tracks—she went towards the communicating door. The key was in her side and she turned it, giving a slight knock as she twisted the handle and pressed the door open.

'I can't get the safety chain unfastened,' she said.

Rafaello was standing by his tallboy, slipping his cufflinks from his dress shirt. His jacket was abandoned and his bow tie untied, the top button of his shirt undone. He turned at her abrupt entry. Turned and stilled.

Alaina had stilled too. Absently, in her mind, words ran. What *was* it about a man in evening dress with his bow tie loose and his top button undone? It should be nothing…nothing at all! And yet—

She gulped silently. Oh, dear God, but he looked so…so…

'Come here.' He held a hand out to her. 'You'll need to stand by the light.'

He was under one of the wall sconces, where the pooling light enhanced the play of shadow across him.

Numbly, she walked towards him. This had been a bad, bad idea…

But she walked towards him all the same.

He took her shoulder, turned her lightly, stood behind her so the light from the wall sconce was shining down on the nape of her neck.

'Hold still.'

She held still. She could do nothing else *but* hold still. Except in every cell of her body that same faint tremor that had been set off when he had taken her into his arms to dance with her was set off again. And she could not stop it, or calm it, nor do anything about it at all.

She felt his fingers, cool and expert, brush her loosened hair over one shoulder, then release the tricky safety catch…felt the necklace sag forward. She caught it with her fingers, turning to hold it out to him.

'Please, Rafaello, keep it. It's too valuable for me to want it in my room.'

He took it absently, dropping it as if it were nothing more than costume jewellery from a market stall on top of his tallboy. His attention was not on the diamond necklace, but on her. On her silky dressing gown with its silver facings.

'I remember this,' he said. There was a husk beneath the cool murmur of his voice, and his eyelids had drooped. 'You had it on the island. I admired its effect then, as I recall. I also recall…' before she had time to realise what he was doing, his hand had dropped to her waist, was drawing at the tie of the belt '…relieving you of it…'

She couldn't move. It was as if every nerve in her body were paralysed.

'Rafaello—no—'

Her voice was faint, a thread. But she could feel her heart rate rocket. Protest rose. And then panic.

I didn't come in here for this—I didn't...

Her eyes flew to his, dismay flooding her. That look in his face, in his eyes, that glint of gold so distinct within their hooded depths, the faint curve of his mouth....

I don't want this.

She heard the words again in her head. But they were fainter now. Drowned by the thudding of her heart, by the heat suddenly, disastrously, rising up in her.

'No?'

A lift of his eyebrow, his voice low and husky...quizzical. She felt his hand pause.

'Are you sure, Alaina? Are you really, really sure?'

Yes!

The single essential word shouted in her head. She was as sure as she had been on the moonlit terrace at the villa when he'd kissed her. Nothing had changed—*nothing!* She must go...must step away, walk away, go back to the communicating door, back into her bedroom, shut the door behind her, lock it...

But she did not move. Could not move. Could do nothing at all except, in a voice that was so faint it was a sigh, a whisper, say his name. Only that.

'Rafaello...'

She felt herself sway—a movement without conscious volition, a kind of instinct beyond her control. Beyond reason.

'Alaina...'

He echoed his name with hers, and she could hear in it… Not humour…no, not that.

Desire.

He drew her towards him, folding her against him, and his mouth found hers lifted to him. Like the softest silk… like the richest velvet…his mouth moved on hers. Faintness drummed through her, and so much more.

Then, at her waist, she felt his hand slip the belt of her dressing gown, loosening it from her.

And she was lost…

She was naked in his arms, her warm, silken body pressed against his.

With effortless ease he lifted her up, carried her to his waiting bed.

Past and present fused.

He laid her down on the waiting sheets, his breath catching. Her naked beauty inflamed him, and he felt his body surge, desire coursing through him. But he held it back, held it in check. He must not rush her.

He lowered himself beside her, sitting on the bed, leaning over her, for a moment simply gazing down at her. Her eyes, wide and distended, clung to his. He said her name again—a low, hushed murmur. Then reached his hand forward.

Slowly, intently, he touched her breasts, the warm, soft mounds silken against his palm. They flowered at his touch, and a low, aroused moan came from her throat. He lifted his hand away. Replaced it with his lips. Slowly, sensuously, he laved the coral peaks, hearing that low moan come again. He heard his name, and then her hands were curving around his back, seeking to draw him down to her.

He felt the impediment of his clothes with a sudden impatient rush. He jack-knifed up, shedding them swiftly, disposing of them as unnecessary hindrances to what he now most wanted in all the world. Then he returned to the bed where she lay waiting for him, as she had lain and waited for him before—so many times. Each time in the overture to a night of passion and of pleasure.

As tonight would be…

He came down beside her, his body rich and ripe with desire. More than his body… How beautiful she was. How much he wanted her. Wanted her to want him…

And she did. He could see it in her face, in her dilated eyes holding his, alight with all that he wanted there to be in them. He could hear it in the quickening of her breathing, feel it in her exquisite, engorged, coral-tipped breasts, the slight but oh-so-telling slackening of her thighs.

Her hands reached up to him to wind around his waist and draw him to her. His mouth closed over hers, his body moved over hers, his own arousal surging. She was warm and soft and silken, her mouth tender beneath his, her lips parting as his kiss deepened to feast on all that she was offering. His body pressed on hers and he felt her thighs widen under his, felt her give a gasp, low in her throat, as she felt the strength of his manhood.

Still he held back, memory possessing him. He was recalling how she liked to make love…just what it was that he could do to her that would bring her body to wild thrashing, make her voice cry out in sensual ecstasy.

His mouth lifted from her, gliding down the contour of her throat, beneath the sweet valley of her ripened breasts, over the satin slenderness of her waist and further still, lower now, to where she was most achingly sensitive. His hands held her flanks, his mouth and his lips skimming her with arousing caress. Her hands had slid caressingly up the strong column of his back, and her fingernails were indenting now on his shoulders. He felt her back straining to arch beneath him.

She said his name, helpless, pleading, as he readied her for his possession, wanting her desire to reach its peak so that the pleasure he would give her would soar above his own. He lifted his mouth away and she gave a cry, as if of loss, but then he was moving his body up over hers again, his mouth finding hers, fusing her lips with his in the mounting passion between them.

His arousal quickened, urgency filling him. She, too, was quickening, her thighs pressing against his, widening under his, and her spine was arching again, hips lifting to his.

It was an invitation that he could not refuse…that was impossible to refuse. She was saying his name again, through the passion of their kisses, and he knew the moment had come—the moment was now…*now…*

He entered her without hesitation, with a hunger that sought its own satiation, and she cried out, her hands coming down to his hips, pressing him, pulling him against her, more deeply into her. He thrust forward, feeling their bodies fuse, and it was right, so right, for them to do so. He folded her into him, felt the delicate tissues of her body embracing him, taking him deeper…deeper yet.

And then he felt her body flame all around him, felt her convulse in sudden, throbbing pulsation, heard her cry out, more wildly now, in an ecstasy that was almost anguish. Her hands snaked around his back, either side of his spine, pressing and splaying as if she would never let him go, would hold him within her for ever.

He said her name, ragged and beyond control, his head

lifted, thrown back, as all through his body the power of his own moment forged through him. Absolute possession. Absolute fusion. Absolute union of their bodies. Shuddering through him, taking him, and her, to the apotheosis of desire fulfilled, sated and consumed.

For an ageless moment he was blinded by it, possessed by it, then slowly...very slowly...he felt his body subside. Grow heavy and lax. He could feel little whorls of pleasure still echoing in her body, tangible to him, and smiled to feel them. With a shaking hand he smoothed the dampened tendrils of her hair. She was gazing up at him with the same blindness, the same wonder.

He kissed her softy, gently, but the need for sleep was drumming through him...the body's exhaustion, the mind's oblivion. He said her name again, slipping from her only to fold her close against him, against the hectic beating of his heart. Her softness, her tenderness, was all that he craved now.

His last barely conscious thought, before oblivion took him, was that he knew with a certainty that filled every cell in his body that reclaiming her, making her his own again, was all that he had wanted it to be...could ever want it to be...

Past fused with present, and present with past—and *now* was what was good. So very, very good...

Then sleep took him as she was held fast in his arms. The only place he wanted her to be.

Alaina stretched languorously in the dawn light, one thigh warm against Rafaello's. Memory, familiarity and a wonderful sense of happiness suffused her. It was as if those five long years since she had last lain like this alongside Rafaello, their bodies intertwined so sensually, had never been.

Words, inchoate, welling up from deep within her still drowsing consciousness, formed in her mind.

I belong here...

She slid her arm around his lean waist, wrapping herself to him, one cheek on his hard, smooth chest, her long hair trailing over him as he slept.

She hovered between waking and drowsing and more words formed, silent but sibilant in her mind.

This is right—this is how it should be.

She had been right—oh, so right—to abandon her struggle to resist him and to yield to what she knew, despite all her verbal denials to him, she wanted...

What she had wanted from the moment Rafaello had walked back into her life, reigniting that old flame...

How could she quench it again? Five years ago she had had to. Five years ago he had wanted her no longer...had taken his leave of her. Left her life for good.

But now he was back in it—and she was back in his.

And he wanted her.

Not just as the mother of the child they had unintentionally conceived—the little boy who had lit up her life, who was an undeserved gift and so, so precious. And surely she should be glad—and grateful, and relieved—that Rafaello wanted Joey! Wanted to be in his life.

A sliver of cold went through her. Rafaello might have rejected Joey, wanted nothing to do with him, played no part in his life. Might have considered him a burden, unwelcome and unacknowledged. That was what she had feared five years ago, on discovering her affair with Rafaello had left her pregnant.

But her fears had proved groundless. Rafaello had not

hesitated—had not questioned or doubted or delayed. He had rearranged his entire life so that Joey could be part of it. Joey...the son he wanted.

And he wants me too—wants me as he wanted me on the island.

And she wanted him to want her—wanted to want him. She knew that now, with a certainty that filled her.

She felt him stir, felt the arm around her shoulder tighten, drawing her closer to him, felt his other hand reach to rest on her rounded hip. She heard him murmur something in Italian, soft and fluid. Then his body relaxed again and he lapsed into sleep once more.

Drowsiness, sated and sensual, eased through her, and her thoughts and her consciousness faded. She let the dark, and the night, and the warmth of Rafaello's embrace, draw her back down into sweet, honeyed slumber. Happiness and gladness suffused her, and she had only one last drowsy thought.

How good it was to be here in his arms again...how very, very good...

It was the right place for her to be. So, so right...

CHAPTER NINE

RAFAELLO GLANCED BRIEFLY in his rear-view mirror. Alaina was sitting beside Joey in the back of the car, reading a story to him as they sped along the autostrada leading south out of Rome. They were heading to Amalfi, and Rafaello was not looking forward to reaching their destination.

He was taking Joey and Alaina to meet his father.

He'd written to inform his father of his marriage as soon as they'd arrived in Italy, knowing it would not be welcome news. But his father had merely indicated he should visit, and now they were. But it was a duty visit, nothing more. He already knew what his father would say.

Trapped you, did she? You should have known better! At least tell me the prenup is watertight!

Would he be interested in Joey? Oh, not in the boy himself—Rafaello knew that with the unsentimental clarity engendered in him by his own upbringing; his father hadn't taken much interest in his own son while young— but as his grandson, his genetic progeny?

He shrugged mentally. His father's interest, or lack of it, would make little impact on Joey, or indeed on Rafaello either. If his mother had still been alive, though…

He pulled his mind away. That was not something

he wanted to think about either. If his father would be predominantly indifferent to Joey's existence, he knew his mother would have been over-emotional and over-indulgent, possessive and neurotic, with an excess of sensibility...

No, he did not wish to dwell on that. It was all so long ago. The past was gone, and it was the present he must focus on. The present which, he thought, his mood mellowing as he cruised along the busy autostrada, had so much to commend it.

His glance went to the rear-view mirror again. Alaina's head was turned towards Joey, delineating her lovely profile, and he felt his mood improve yet more. Since the night she had come to him after the dinner-dance, every night had been as good. There was no holding back, no reluctance or questioning or denial of what had been rekindled between them. She was as ardent, as eager, as he could wish. And he was glad of it—very, very glad.

And that was a good feeling to have. Surprisingly so...

His life, which the discovery of Joey's existence had turned upside down, was settling again. Running, once again, on smooth, oiled wheels, with nothing to disrupt or unsettle it again. He had Joey, the son he was doing his best to be a father to, and he had Alaina, whose beauty aroused him as strongly as it once had. Their desire was rekindled—and now there was no reason for that flame to be extinguished.

No reason at all...

Joey was restless, bored with the long car journey. And there was still about another half an hour to go before they reached their destination.

Alaina felt tension dart within her. She was not exactly looking forward to this visit. Rafaello's father did not sound like an easy man.

Not that she had said as much to Rafaello. She understood this was a necessary visit—introducing her and Joey to Rafaello's surviving parent. Severino Ranieri was supposedly retired—but, as Rafaello had made clear to her, he still kept a sharp eye on the family firm, even though these days it was run by Rafaello himself.

'My father speaks his mind,' Rafaello had informed her. 'He knows the circumstances of our marriage, obviously, but what he will make of Joey I am unsure. He will be glad of a grandson—an heir, so to speak, to continue the family line. But—'

'But less glad of me,' Alaina had finished drily.

Rafaello had glanced at her. 'He will be civil to you,' he had said.

'And I,' she had replied, 'will be civil to him in return.'

But for all her assurances, when the introductions were made on their arrival at the imposing-looking residence in an affluent region of the dramatic Amalfi coastline, she was on her guard.

Rafaello's father was tall, like him, and good-looking, in a severe fashion, even in his seventies. But, she thought, his distinguished appearance did not hide the chill in his eyes. If Rafaello presented his keen intelligence within an outwardly smooth, urbane manner, his father was more like a blade with its cutting edge unconcealed.

'So.' Severino's tone was clipped, as he addressed his son. 'This is your…unexpected wife and son.'

His inexpressive glance went briefly to Alaina, then dropped to where Joey stood beside her, holding her hand.

'Well, no point questioning his paternity,' he remarked. His eyes went back to Alaina. 'You will wish to refresh yourself after your journey. My housekeeper will attend to you. Rafaello, a word...'

He indicated that his son should follow him, leaving Alaina to be shown upstairs, with Joey trotting beside her, looking about him interestedly, by a timid-looking middle-aged woman.

Joey was asking questions, and Alaina answered as best she could.

'Yes, the elderly gentleman is your grandfather,' she said. 'And, like I told you, because he's elderly, you will need to be quiet, darling. He won't like a lot of noise or excitement.'

And that was not all that Rafaello's father would not like—that was obvious. But she kept that to herself. Welcoming he had *not* been. As to whether he would even be civil was questionable. It was perfectly clear he would have preferred her and Joey not to exist at all.

Well, that was no concern of hers. The timid-looking housekeeper was showing her into a guest bedroom, indicating the en suite bathroom, where she could make use of the facilities. Alaina was glad they were not staying with Rafaello's father, but were booked into a hotel nearby. All she had to get through was lunch, some conversation—however stilted—and then they could leave.

Even so, lunch was not a relaxing affair. Joey, mindful of her admonition, was on his best behaviour, and was looking smart in long trousers and a shirt with a little waistcoat, his hair neatly brushed. He got a measured, unsmiling look from the man who was his grandfather. She got one as well.

Alaina suspected he was pricing her outfit—a stylish designer two-piece in pale green, purchased in the Via

Condotti—and, she surmised, thinking she had done well out of marrying his son.

The conversation, conducted in English, centred on herself. And it was less of a conversation than a cross-examination.

Alaina answered the clearly leading questions composedly.

'Yes, Rafaello and I met on holiday. It was a relationship that was not intended to last. I chose to be a single mother for that reason. However, Rafaello, meeting me again by chance, convinced me that a two-parent family was preferable—hence my presence now, in Italy and in his life. That's all there is to it really,' she said, calmly continuing to eat.

'Indeed,' Rafaello's father said tightly.

'Indeed...' echoed Rafaello.

Alaina could hear the ironic timbre in his voice. It drew a sharp glance from his father and a swift utterance in rapid Italian that she could not understand and was probably glad not to. Whatever it was—and she had a shrewd idea that it was not complimentary about herself—it drew no response from Rafaello. He was, she could see, indifferent to it. Or at least appearing to be so.

His father reverted to English. 'You have legitimised the boy?'

He put the question to Rafaello.

'As I told you, yes.'

Rafaello's reply was as composed as hers had been.

His father's mouth tightened. 'It will never be as satisfactory as a child born in wedlock,' he remarked.

'We are not a dynasty,' Rafaello replied, his manner seeming still unruffled by his father's implied criticism. 'There is no title or nobility to be affected.'

'Nevertheless, it is not a desirable situation.'

The chilly eyes flickered over Alaina again, with a dismissive expression in them, and then returned to Rafaello.

'But what is done is done.' He reached for his wine. 'I can only be relieved that your mother is not with us any longer. Her emotionality would have been tiresome in the extreme.' His glance now went to his grandson, dutifully and silently eating his food. 'She would have spoilt the boy completely!'

Alaina smiled sweetly, and decided to intervene. 'But that is the role of a *nonna*. It is sad that Joey has no grandmothers to make a fuss over him. My own mother died some years ago.'

Sharp eyes came at her. 'And your father?'

'He remarried shortly after her death. I am no longer in contact. He lives in Scotland.'

'And his circumstances?' There was a discernible edge in the terse enquiry.

'Like you, he is retired. He worked as a scientist for one of the government departments.' She paused minutely, taking a sip from her water. 'He is quite respectable,' she said.

Severino Ranieri's face tightened. He did not, it was evident, care to be answered back to—or to have his own assumptions called out.

Thoughts ran through her head as she resumed eating. Rafaello might have inherited his father's good looks and his keen intelligence, but that was all—and Alaina was glad of it.

Severino Ranieri made another remark in Italian to his son, and even though she did not understand it completely, she caught enough to know that he was making a waspish comment about women and sharp tongues. As before, Rafaello made no answer.

Alaina decided she had had enough of this not so covert inquisition.

'I am looking forward to seeing something of this dramatic part of Italy,' she declared. 'Though I'm not sure about Pompeii and Herculaneum—probably best to wait until Joey is older and at school, learning about the Romans. A boat trip to Capri might be more fun for him. What do you think, Joey darling?'

Joey, still mindful of her previous admonitions to be on his best behaviour, said 'Yes, please, Mummy,' in an ultra good-boy tone.

She smiled, then looked across at Rafaello's father. 'Would you join us?' she asked limpidly.

There was a sound that might have come from Rafaello's throat, but she wasn't looking at him and wasn't sure. His father's face had tightened again.

'I will leave that joy to yourselves,' he answered acerbically.

Alaina hadn't for a moment imagined that he would agree to come, and nor had she wanted him to. A shaft of sadness went through her. She hadn't expected Rafaello's father to be a doting grandfather, but all the same...

As for my father—he doesn't even know Joey exists, and I will never tell him. What for? So he can ignore him as he ignored me all my life? As he ignored my mother?

Severino Ranieri was addressing his son now, and Alaina looked at him. He and her own father were cut from the same cloth. Unemotional, cerebral, self-contained, uncomfortable with emotion.

They don't want other people loving them.

No, that was a dangerous path to go down.

Involuntarily, her gaze went to Rafaello. Tension netted her suddenly. Rafaello was not chilly, like his father, but there was a detachment about him that came across as coolness—a dissociation from the rough and tumble messiness of human affections. As if he were, however urbanely, keeping the world at a distance.

Keeping people at a distance.

Whoever they were.

A troubled expression clouded her eyes. This was the man she had married…the father of her son. The man whose physical appeal to her was overwhelming, and whose bed she now shared. She was no longer fighting what was impossible for her to fight. This was the man who could inflame her with a skilled, sensual passion she could not resist, and yet…

A question was trying to shape itself in her head, but she did not want to allow it do so—let alone answer it. She batted it away, dismissing it. Silencing her disquiet.

There is no need for that question—because there is no purpose to it. We are married, and making a home for Joey, making a sustainable marriage, making something for ourselves as well as for our son. So why think any more about it?

She moved her thoughts away from this dangerous ground.

'So, is Capri overrated?' she asked, addressing the question to both Rafaello and his father.

'It depends what you want,' Rafaello answered smoothly. 'It's extremely popular, as you know. I expect Joey will enjoy the boat ride.'

Rafaello's father looked at him disapprovingly. 'You must not over-indulge him,' he said.

Alaina felt herself bristle, but banked it down—there was no point in reacting to her father-in-law.

She saw Rafaello's expression become veiled.

'Definitions of over-indulgence may vary,' he replied. His tone was as veiled as his expression.

His father moved on to another line of criticism.

'What is happening about his schooling? It should not be delayed by his lack of Italian.'

Alaina got her reply in before Rafaello. 'He'll be starting in the autumn term at the infant class of the International School near the villa Rafaello has taken.'

Cold eyes rested on her. 'School is good for children—and not just for their education. It makes them independent of any maternal possessiveness.' His glance went to Rafaello. 'For you that was essential,' he said.

That veiled look was on Rafaello's face once more... inexpressive. Alaina was glad that the housekeeper came in at that point, to remove their plates and set down a platter of cheeses and biscuits. Rafaello made some genial remark to the housekeeper, and Alaina saw the woman's face light up. But then her employer made a terse remark and the frightened expression reappeared. Alaina merely thanked her as she took her and Joey's empty plates away.

Clearly cheese was instead of any dessert course, and Alaina selected a mild-tasting one for Joey, with a couple of biscuits, taking a sliver for herself of something that looked like Camembert—more out of politeness than anything else.

Conversation limped on, stilted and formal, with her polite enquires about the Amalfi region receiving only clipped replies from her father-in-law, ameliorated by Rafaello's more expansive ones. Joey, she could see with a sense of foreboding, was running out of ultra good-boy mode and getting restless.

Her attention would keep his restlessness at bay, she knew, and she left the conversation to Rafaello and his father, who reverted to Italian. A covert glance told her that neither father nor son were at ease. She wondered if Severino Ranieri even knew the meaning of the word.

A sense of depression edged over her. Rafaello's father was, indeed, cut from the same severe, unyielding material as her own father. It was a blessing Rafaello was not like that.

Yet there were elements of that in him. She knew she had to acknowledge that. He made no accommodations when his course was set. He'd placed those stark options before her—to marry him or face a court battle over Joey. Memory stabbed at her. Five years ago, on their last day together on the island, he had had closed down the conversation she'd tried to have with him about whether their time together must really be over.

'We each have our own lives to lead,' he had said.

He had not said it harshly, or coldly, but he had meant it…

Her expression shadowed.

And now our lives have come together again—because of Joey.

Emotion plucked at her, but she could not identify it. Did not want to. It was dangerous to do so. Much better to pay it no attention, not to address it or give it entrance. Much better to accept the life she was now leading.

I have Joey and I have Rafaello. All I could possibly want.

That was good—very good indeed. So very, very good…

Rafaello was getting to his feet, his father likewise.

Rafaello looked at Alaina. 'I think we must make a move,' he said.

Relieved, she stood up too, telling Joey they were going now.

They took their leave, with the poor housekeeper holding open the front door, and Alaina smiled her thanks as she went out, holding Joey's hand. They all got back into the car that was parked on the carriage sweep and Alaina settled Joey into his child seat, strapping him in as Rafaello got into the driving seat and gunned the engine.

She looked back to the front door, expecting to see his father there, bidding them goodbye, but it was already shut.

She said nothing, and nor did Rafaello. But was there a tenseness across his shoulders and in the stiffness of his neck as they drove off the property and on to the highway? She wasn't sure, but she could well understand if there was. She herself felt as if she could finally breathe easily.

She made no remark about their visit, though, only saying brightly, 'How far to the hotel?'

'A few kilometres,' came the answer. Rafaello's tone was short.

She said no more, busying herself pointing out the passing scenery to Joey. He was getting sleepy, she could see, especially now he was back in the car, and she let him doze off. Rafaello still didn't speak, but she let him be.

At the hotel—an old-fashioned but luxurious-looking edifice perched atop a steep cliffside—they checked in and went up to their room. Joey had surfaced, and was becoming chatty again, but it was only Alaina who answered his questions and acknowledged his observations.

The afternoon was still warm, though the sun was

lowering over the azure sea gloriously on view from their balcony.

'Mummy, there's a swimming pool!' Joey said excitedly, pointing down to where he had spotted a rectangular patch of blue set in the gardens, sparkling in the sunshine.

'You two go down,' Rafaello said. 'I'll follow. I must check on some work matters.'

He was getting out his laptop, setting it on the desk. The tense look was still evident and, again, Alaina let him be. He needed time on his own. And she… Well, the pool looked just as enticing to her as it did Joey.

She threw open the lid of her suitcase and rummaged for their swimming gear, extracting it, then quickly changing Joey into swim shorts and a tee, and herself into a one-piece with a sundress over the top. She grabbed sandals for their feet, and a tube of suncream for them both.

'We're off,' she said cheerfully to Rafaello, who barely looked up from his laptop.

He had a closed, focussed expression on his face, his eyes scanning a document on the screen.

She set off with Joey, who was tugging her along eagerly. Ultra good-boy mode had vanished, and she, too, felt that she'd just come off duty. Daughter-in-law duty, which was supposed to have shown her presence in Rafaello's life as something other than a gold-digging adventuress foisting her bastard son on Severino's family.

But she wasn't angry about it. She'd learnt long ago that anger achieved nothing. Had learnt that lesson as her father's daughter. She could remember trying to convince her mother that both anger and tears were pointless.

It's not his fault, Mum. He doesn't possess the faculty for love. It's missing in him. All we can do is not love him ourselves. That's the only protection we can have.

Sadness filled her. It had been easier for her, she knew, to survive without her father's love. But not for her mother.

She just went on craving it…all her life. Desperate for him to love her back. And he never would, and never could—it wasn't in him.

She stepped with Joey into the elevator, letting him press the button as he loved to do.

As the car plunged down, it took her stomach with it. Echoing the plunging emotion that was stabbing at her.

Never fall for a man who does not and cannot love you back.

It was the warning she'd lived by all her life, thanks to her mother's sad and sorry example of the fate awaiting any woman who made that fatal mistake.

A warning she must never forget…

It had saved her…*just*…on the island. And it must keep her safe now.

What I have to do now with Rafaello is only to make our marriage workable, for Joey's sake.

That was all she must allow.

CHAPTER TEN

RAFAELLO WALKED OUT on to the pool deck. The hotel was not full, and he could see Joey and Alaina, the pool's sole occupants at this late hour of the afternoon, disporting themselves in the water. A large degree of splashing was involved.

He gave an involuntary smile. Out of nowhere, he felt the tension that had netted him since the morning suddenly evaporate finally. His duty visit to his father had been necessary, but an ordeal. Now he and Alaina, and Joey, could have the rest of the weekend to themselves.

Joey caught sight of him and called out excitedly.

'Mummy and me are having a splashing competition! I'm winning!'

Rafaello let his eyes rest on the little boy, who was back to splashing frantically at Alaina, who was ducking exaggeratedly. They were at the shallow end, Alaina standing, Joey buoyant in his water wings.

Memory shafted in him—or rather an absence of memory. His mother had disliked the water, and they had had no pool anyway, nor gone on beach holidays. Their holidays, such as they were, had been walking holidays, up in the Dolomites. His father had led the way, striding wordlessly forward, his mother next, fearful of falling, but insistent on coming along anyway, desperate to do anything her husband might want to do, and not to be excluded. As for himself, he'd plodded along in their wake, not expecting to enjoy any of it.

There was little of his boyhood that he'd enjoyed at all. School—boarding school, as soon as he could be despatched by his father, who had been insistent on getting him away from the baleful influence of his neurotic mother—had been a respite. There he had made his select friends, discovered that being intelligent gained the teachers' approval. And being good at sports such as fencing and climbing had given gave him sufficient social cachet not to be written off as a nerd.

In his teenage years he'd discovered that good looks and a cool manner served him well too. His cool manner had predominated, keeping both his father's implied criticism and his mother's neurotic clinginess at bay. It had also, he knew, made him attractive to females keen to get past that air of dispassionate reserve, which he'd punctuated with smooth attentiveness when he'd felt like it, for those females he'd considered qualified for his interest in them. All had been keen to be selected by him for such affairs as he was prepared to indulge in when the occasion had suited him.

Such as on the island, with Alaina.

And now...?

Well, now choice had been removed from the situation. Not for a moment would he have reneged on his responsibilities towards the child Alaina had borne him. Did he wish she hadn't? An irrelevant question. He dealt in realities—anything else was pointless. And this reality came with distinct advantages.

His eyes rested on Alaina now, on the way the sleek

one-piece moulded her figure, the way the water lapped her breasts in a very pleasing manner. He found his mood lifting more. Found himself wishing he had not reserved a family room but a suite, wondering if it could be changed at this late hour. But even in an adjoining room, if |Joey did not settle then there would be no point.

Just as there had been no point thinking that his father would have been any different today than the way he had always been. Alaina had coped well—he must congratulate her. As for Joey...

His smile quirked at his mouth. Joey most definitely deserved a treat for his ultra good-boy performance!

He shrugged off his short-sleeved, open-necked shirt and shucked off his pool shoes.

'Time to even the score,' he informed Joey, who was still mercilessly batting water at his mother.

He slid into the pool, welcoming the cool water lapping at his thighs.

Joey gave a cry of excited glee, paddling frantically in his direction, splashing mightily as he did so. Rafaello fisted both hands and brought them crashing down into the water, sending out a mini tsunami towards Joey. Joey shrieked and battle commenced.

In his head, Rafaello heard his father's admonition not to over-indulge Joey.

The sound of splashing water drowned it out.

Or something did.

Rafaello did not trouble himself to listen to it again...

That night they decided to dine on their balcony, making use of Room Service. Joey, sufficiently tired out by a lot of fun in the pool, was fast asleep in his little bed inside.

He'd had his supper out by the pool—a large helping of pasta, followed by a bowl of ice-cream.

Out on the horizon the sun had set. Lights were pricking on along the coastline and out on the sea itself, from fishing boats and night cruisers. It was still warm, but not so warm that Alaina did not welcome the light shawl around her shoulders.

Rafaello had a cotton sweater knotted around his neck, over an open-necked shirt with the cuffs turned back, and wore dark blue chinos that matched her own navy-blue cotton trousers and elbow length top. She hadn't bothered with make-up, just washed her hair after its immersion in the pool, and was now letting it dry by itself, scooped off her forehead with a hairband. Rafaello hadn't shaved, given the informality of their dining.

'Very piratical,' Alaina observed as they took their places at the little table on the balcony as Room Service departed, leaving dinner tucked under covered serving dishes.

Rafaello rubbed his darkening jawline ruminatively. 'Not a good image for a lawyer,' he remarked.

'You'd have to grow it into a proper beard—that would lend appropriate gravitas. Maybe when you hit fifty?' she suggested. 'You might be a judge by then!'

He laughed. 'Not my line of the law,' he replied.

She reached for her glass of wine, taking a considering sip. 'I could see your father as a judge,' she said. 'Though I wouldn't like to come up against him when it came to sentencing.'

'He'd be the type to throw the book at you,' Rafaello agreed. He took a mouthful of his wine, then set it back on the table, looking directly at Alaina. 'Thank you for coping with him as well as you did today.'

She gave a demurring, brief smile. 'Thank my train-ing in the hospitality business! We are taught to handle difficult hotel guests by being the three Cs—calm, com-posed and collected. Don't argue, merely state, and stay polite at all times, whatever the provocation.'

Rafaello's eyes glinted. 'You lapsed only once,' he re-plied. 'Telling him your father was "quite respectable".'

She made a face. 'Guilty as charged.' Her expression changed. 'They're very alike,' she said slowly. 'Aloof is probably the best one-word description.'

Rafaello looked at her. 'You said you were no longer in touch with him.'

He reached for their plates on the serving trolley be-side them, lifting the domed covers away and placed hers in front of her, doing the same with his own. The *primo* was a seafood salad, and Alaina got stuck in, glad they were not facing another gruelling meal with Rafaello's disapproving father.

'No,' she said. 'There didn't seem much point. He re-married within six months of my mother's death, and I went off to college. I didn't go to his wedding—it seemed far too hypocritical to do so, given the rapidity with which he had remarried. I've never met his second wife. She was a colleague, he told me, when he informed me he was marrying again and they were moving to Scotland. She's a scientist too, so probably better suited to him than my mother was.'

Rafaello was silent for a moment, making a start on his own *primo*.

'Curious that we both have parents who were not suited to each other,' he said. 'Why did yours marry in the first place?'

'My mother was in love with him. She thought...'

Alaina could hear the edge to her voice '…thought that she could break through his aloofness. But she couldn't.' Her voice changed. 'I've always thought that she sort of bled to death from her heart—'

She broke off, reached for her wine.

'What about your parents?' she challenged. 'Why did *they* marry?'

'My mother's family was wealthy and socially well connected. She was a good match for my father in that respect. But…'

He paused, and Alaina knew why, for it echoed her own pause.

'But because she was very beautiful, and a social butterfly, she was used to being adored by men. My father was the exception. She only irritated him. So she focussed all her emotions on me instead.'

His voice had become expressionless. But he continued, all the same.

'My father found that irritating too, and he disapproved of it. So he sent me off to boarding school to remove me from her malign influence.'

Alaina was silent for a moment. 'My father did the opposite. He left me to my mother. He himself ignored me…just as he ignored my mother.' She frowned. 'Had I been a boy, perhaps, or even if I had been scholarly— especially if I'd turned out to have a yen for science—he might have paid some attention to me. But…' she gave a slight shrug, as she had shrugged off, long ago, her father's indifference to her existence '…as it was, he had no reason to be interested in me.'

She pushed her now-empty plate aside, reached for her wine again.

She looked across at Rafaello. 'I've come to terms with it long since. I don't let it affect or upset me any longer.'

She said the words, but they plucked at her all the same. It wasn't her own relationship with her father that upset her—it was her mother's. The lesson her mother's fate had taught her. Never to love when it was not returned... when it could never be returned. When it was impossible that it should be so.

She took another sip of her wine, then set down her glass.

'I was eighteen when my mother died—she was knocked down by a car. How...how old were you?'

'Twenty-three. I'd just qualified as a lawyer. My father was pleased with me. Though he was less pleased when he learnt I was going to visit my mother at her clinic.'

Alaina frowned. 'Clinic?'

'Yes.' Rafaello's manner was calm, and he lifted her empty plate, along with his, placing them on the trolley, then handing her their *secondo*—a delicately spiced lamb tagine. 'She'd been there a while...my father thought it for the best. Her nerves were not good.' He started to eat, his manner still calm.

'What...what happened?'

'There was some confusion over her medication. It caused an adverse reaction.' He tapped his plate. 'This tagine is excellent. And the wine goes well with it.'

He was changing the subject. Alaina let him. They had both gone into deep waters—time to wade back.

'Yes, both are delicious,' she agreed. 'Tell me, are you OK with going to Capri tomorrow? I think we might have to get out on a boat, at least, as Joey will be disappointed otherwise. But it needn't be to Capri—any boat ride will do!'

In her head she heard Rafaello's father warning against over-indulgence. Her face tightened momentarily, her glance going to Rafaello. His expression was unperturbed.

The three Cs applied to him too, she thought. Calm, composed and collected. Applied constantly really. It was his normal manner. Very little, if anything, ruffled him. He dealt with life rationally. Coolly. Smoothly.

'Let's see how things go,' he said now. 'Capri can always wait. As you say, a boat ride is what Joey will be keen on. And the lift down to the swimming platform.'

The conversation moved on to ways in which Joey would be entertained on the morrow, and then on to the Amalfi coast in general, Vesuvius and its impact on the area.

'As I said at lunch,' Alaina remarked, 'I don't really want to take Joey to Pompeii or Herculaneum. He's too young, and the ruins wouldn't mean much. And, quite frankly, it's too upsetting anyway, thinking back to that nightmare disaster for all those people.'

'Yes,' replied Rafaello, 'it was a cruel fate for them. Nature can be very harsh.'

'People, too,' Alaina heard herself say. 'But...' she frowned '...sometimes they don't mean it—as in, they don't do it intentionally to hurt others. They just lack the capacity to be otherwise.'

She'd moved the subject back to their respective fathers again, and wished she hadn't. Her eyes rested on Rafaello in the dim light. The table lamp was throwing his features into *chiaroscuro* as the evening gathered around them. The play of shadow and illumination seemed to make his features more austere. More like his father's.

Well, they look alike—just as Joey looks like Rafaello. It's natural.

Yet just for an instant she felt uneasy.

Then it dissipated.

Rafaello was making some remark about the likelihood, or not, of Vesuvius erupting again, and how the rich volcanic soil benefited agriculture and viticulture.

'Better harvests to enjoy—but living in the shadow of danger.'

He reached for his wine, and took a leisurely mouthful, the lamplight giving his face a flickering saturnine cast.

'Yes,' Alaina replied. 'There's always a price to pay,' she observed.

Again, for an instant, she heard her own words hanging in the air...

She set them aside. That wasn't a path she was going to take. She was sticking to the safe path, the predictable route. Creating a way for Joey to know his father and for Rafaello to know his son. And for her and Rafaello to enjoy each other, as they had the first time around.

Thinking of which...

Her expression changed. A familiar frisson shaped itself inside her. His rough jawline was really making him very, very attractive right now...

He caught her gaze. Exchanged it for a similar look that changed to one of humour charged with irony and regret.

'We'll have to take a rain check,' he told her, his mouth quirking. 'We can't disturb young Joey's slumber...'

Alaina gave an exaggerated sigh. 'Ah, well, so be it.' She pushed aside her empty plate. 'OK, if that's one appetite I can't indulge, I'll compensate with indulging in a generous *dolce* instead. What do you think is on offer?'

It proved to be a delicious, rich and delightfully sweet *crema*. She demolished hers happily, then sat back, replete. Rafaello poured coffee for them both, and they sat awhile in the still-mild evening, chatting amiably, with the spectacular night view to gaze on and the stars above to dazzle the heavens.

Alaina relaxed back in her chair, contentment filling her.

This is good. This is more than good.

A phrase of Italian drifted through her head.

La dolce vita.

Oh, it was that all right! A very, very sweet life. She had her beloved Joey, she had Rafaello—she had all she could possibly want.

La dolce vita indeed…

Unseen, around the curve of the bay, Vesuvius slumbered. Dormant and safe. For now.

CHAPTER ELEVEN

'AND SO,' RAFAELLO declared with an air of finality, 'they all lived happily ever after. The end.'

He looked down at Joey. He had his arm around his shoulder as he half lay on his bed, propped against the headboard, while Joey snuggled against him, already almost asleep. Rafaello closed the book and set it aside. With his free hand he turned off the bedside light, leaving only the nightlight to illuminate the bedroom. He could see Joey's eyes closing and hear his breathing slow, felt his little body still cradled against him. Warm and trusting.

Memory flickered in him of the way he had wondered, on first discovering Joey's existence, how he would feel being a father—how he should be one to Joey. He'd known he would never be as his own father had been to him... known he would always acknowledge his responsibilities for his son, would be as good a father as he could be. He'd known he would apply patience and attention to him, would do his best.

So, how *did* it feel?

For a while he just went on sitting there, listening to Joey's breathing, feeling the warmth of his pyjama-clad body against his shoulder.

He heard his own question answered as his son leant trustingly against him, sleeping in the crook of his arm.

It felt good.

Good that he should have read the customary bedtime story as he fell asleep beside him—as he always did when he was at the villa. Good simply to be here with him.

Life had settled into a new routine. He usually stayed in Rome during the working week, or went to the airport for his occasional business trips abroad, but sometimes he arranged matters so he could have a couple of days working from the villa remotely. And he spent every weekend either at the villa, as now, or sometimes Alaina would join him in Rome for an evening, and they would either go out, or entertain at the apartment, leaving Joey in the doting care of Maria and Giorgio. They entertained out here at the villa too—and not only his own established friends and acquaintances. Alaina was building a circle of friends too, including women such as Gina Fratelli, and a few other mothers she'd palled up with at the nursery Joey was now attending three mornings a week. Her and Joey's command of Italian was coming along apace. And Joey, as they'd told his father, would be starting at the International School come the autumn.

Everything, Rafaello thought appreciatively, continuing to sit there with Joey's little body soft against him, was really very...

Very...what?

He wasn't sure what it was...what word would describe it. He frowned slightly. Did it really matter what he thought of the life he lived now? There was no alternative possible, so why analyse it? Why examine or scrutinise it?

Of course, one essential ingredient was Alaina's passion for him... His frown dissipated, replaced by a considering glint in his eyes. It had been awakened again so very satisfyingly and it had not abated—and nor had his for her. The glint intensified. He desired her just as much now as on their first night together in Rome all those weeks ago, back at the start of the summer, when he'd shown her how very enjoyable their reunion could be— how essential, in fact, to making their marriage work.

Thoughts flickered in his head. He did not usually find that his desire for a woman lasted this long. He had always been very…careful in his selection. Avoiding any female who wanted more from him than he was prepared to give. His expression changed. Alaina had once been such a female—not wanting their time in the Caribbean to end, wanting their affair to carry on. Perhaps lead to more…

There was an irony, he was suddenly aware, in the fact that now Alaina had got the 'more' she had sought then because of his son's existence…

His frown came again, and a mental dismissal of the intrusive thought. His life…her life too…was as it was. Joey's existence necessitated it. So speculation and memory were equally irrelevant. It was the present that mattered. And right now that meant the evening ahead.

Realising Joey was fast asleep, he eased his arm away, getting carefully to his feet to draw the quilt around him and ensure Mr Teds was snuggled up to him. He walked quietly to the door, opening it, turning to look back at the sleeping infant one last time before stepping out on to the landing, leaving the door ajar and the landing light on. Then he headed downstairs.

'Fast asleep?' Alaina looked up as he went into the sitting room, where she was curled up on one of the sofas, leafing through a magazine.

'Fast asleep,' he confirmed.

He sat himself down beside her. As she usually did, she had placed a bottle of chilled beer and a glass, plus a bottle opener, on the coffee table next to her own glass of white wine. He opened his beer, poured it out, and she reached for her glass, clinking it against his lightly.

'Maria says dinner in ten minutes,' she told him with a smile, taking a sip of her wine.

'Perfect,' Rafaello said, making a start on his beer. He stretched his long legs out. 'How was today?' he asked.

'Play date with Gina's little boy, and then we came home. Joey had his usual lively session in the pool—he's looking forward to having you share in the fun over the weekend! Then we did some number games, made a jigsaw, did a bit of reading… Then he had his tea and you came home. The rest you know. Bath time and bedtime with Papà.' She smiled. 'How was your day?'

'Office, staff meeting…lunch with a client, court appearance appealing a divorce settlement…back to the office, then fighting my way out of the city to make it back here for Joey's bath time,' Rafaello answered. He took another mouthful of his beer, feeling the good of it. 'I am very glad it's the weekend. What have we got planned? Remind me.'

'Lunch party tomorrow—parents and kiddies from the nursery—but dinner just on our own here. Sunday is free. What shall we do? Any preferences?'

'Just…what's that English term…? Chillaxing. That sounds good to me!' Rafaello smiled and helped himself to Alaina's hand. 'Too dull for you?'

She smiled. 'Dull is the last word I'd ever use for spending time with you,' she answered.

He raised her hand to his mouth and brushed it lightly with his lips.

'What an ideal wife you make,' he murmured, his eyes glinting.

Something changed in her eyes. For a moment it disquieted him, then it was gone. Maybe he'd only imagined it.

She slipped her hand from his, setting down her wine glass. 'I'll go and give Maria a hand in the kitchen,' she said.

Her voice was light, and yet…

He watched her get up and leave the room, her walk as graceful as ever. The evening stretched ahead of him very pleasantly indeed. They would enjoy a well-cooked dinner *à deux*, chatting about whatever it was they usually found it so easy to chat about, and then, assuming Joey didn't wake—which he seldom did—they would have a nightcap out on the terrace.

And then he would take Alaina to bed and they would make love very pleasurably indeed.

Very pleasurably.

He took another easy sip of his beer, savouring the chill and the flavour…the sense of the end of the working week. The sense of an enjoyable weekend underway.

His mind worked contemplatively as he flexed his ankles, drinking his beer unhurriedly. His thoughts went back to what he had contemplated upstairs as Joey had fallen asleep. Since discovering Joey's existence his life had changed fundamentally. The question was…

Do I regret it?

The answer came back the same. That choice had not been possible. So therefore regret or no regret was irrelevant. He had an unavoidable obligation to shoulder the responsibilities that came with his son and he had always honoured his obligations in his life, even conflicting ones. He had been the son his father had wanted him to be, but he had done his best by his mother, too—as much as he'd been able to.

Right to the very end he had at least tried to be patient with her—as his father had not—but he had always known that she craved so much more than he was able to give her. He had held back for his own protection and self-defence. And once he'd reached his teenage years, his young adulthood, he had been as kind as he could, but keeping an essential *cordon sanitaire* between them. Accepting that the situation was as it was, and nothing could change it.

Just as he had now accepted his current situation.

He downed the last of his beer, setting the glass back on the coffee table with a click. Life, after all, was seldom black and white—his clients' convoluted affairs told him that. There were rights and wrongs on both sides all too frequently, and his path was stepping carefully between them towards whatever outcome best benefited whoever was paying his fees.

And the life he now had to take on most definitely came with very clear compensations...

He felt his expression change. A half-smile tugged at his mouth.

Getting to know Joey meant getting to enjoy Alaina.

He got to his feet. Time for dinner.

As he headed towards the dining room, taking the open bottle of white wine with him, he gave a mental nod. His life had changed direction, but it was once again running smoothly.

The way he liked it to be.

Alaina glanced across the table at Rafaello. She was glad he was back for the weekend, and had arrived in time to see Joey before bed. That quiet, end-of-day reading time was important for their bonding. It wasn't something her own father had ever bothered with, and she'd bet that Rafaello's grim father hadn't either, with his son.

Rafaello, she thought sadly, didn't really have anything of a role model when it came to fatherhood—he was having to learn from scratch.

And *was* he bonding with Joey? She could only hope so. Because with Rafaello it was so hard to tell. He kept himself so…

She tried to think of the word that described Rafaello's character. She could come up with *private*, or *elusive*, or *unreadable*, but none of those really fitted him. He was always cordial, pleasant, unruffled, good-humoured, charming, co-operative—there were any number of complimentary adjectives she could use about him, both in the way he was with Joey and with her.

It was just that…

Again, she drew a blank. And as she watched him chat pleasantly with Maria, setting out the dishes, there really was nothing she could criticise him for. With Joey he was always attentive and patient, and with her… A slight blush rose up her cheeks. As a lover he could not be faulted! She melted for him…just *melted*…

And afterwards he would gather her still-trembling body into his arms, smooth her tumbled hair, kiss her softly, hold her in his embrace. He was sensitive, caring, considerate…

Everything a lover should be…

But he's not my lover. He's my husband.

Her eyes shadowed. Yes, Rafaello was her husband—but only because of Joey. Not for any other reason.

Thoughts glided across her head as if on ice…ice that

was dangerously thin. She needed to get off that ice lest it crack beneath her...

Maria was bustling out of the dining room and Rafaello was refilling her wine glass with crisp white wine, filling his own glass too. The *antipasto* before them looked appetising: slivers of fresh melon and mint with finest *prosciutto*, garnished with a delicately fragrant raspberry vinaigrette.

She started on her portion, making some absent reply to the comment Rafaello had just made.

Rafaello—her husband.

And my lover.

Again, she felt the thin ice beneath her. Husband... lover—did it make any difference?

Confusion filled her, and a deep reluctance to let such thoughts, such questions, have any place in her mind. In Amalfi she had called the life she was leading with Rafaello *la dolce vita*...and that was still true. Because what else could it be? She had Joey, she had Rafaello, and life was surely very sweet indeed.

'Alaina?'

Rafaello's quizzical voice recalled her to the moment. She blinked, refocussing. 'Sorry—I missed that completely,' she said.

He gave a slight smile as he started on the *antipasto*. 'Run me through who's turning up for lunch tomorrow,' he said.

She did so, giving him a thumbnail sketch of each of their guests and their offspring who would be there to play with Joey. As she did, her thoughts—incongruously—went to Joey's nursery playmate in England. She ought to invite Ryan to come out...bring Betsy with him for a little holiday. She frowned slightly. But maybe that might be unsettling for Joey—remind him of a life that was no more. And besides… She doubted Rafaello would care for her playing host to an unattached male, even if she and Ryan did go back a long way and between them there had only ever been friendship, nothing more.

No, best leave Ryan and Betsy in the past. Leave her former life in England in the past. Her future was here, in Italy. With Rafaello.

Her gaze went to him now, and softened as it always did when she looked at him.

I thought I would never see him again. Thought our ways had parted for ever. And now…

Now he was an indissoluble part of her life.

She felt emotion rise within her.

I have everything I could ever want.

And surely she had— because what else could she want? What could she possibly lack?

She let the question hang there, floating. Putting no weight on it. Wanting it to drift away, dissipate. Leave her to enjoy this sweet, sweet life she had. Here, like this, with Rafaello.

And to want nothing more…nothing more at all.

CHAPTER TWELVE

'IT'S A LONG DRIVE,' Rafaello was saying, 'but we'll do plenty of stops along the way, Joey.'

'Lom-bard-ee,' said Joey in a sing-song voice, as Rafaello eased the car along the villa's gravelled drive and out on to the highway.

'That's right,' he confirmed. 'Right in the north of Italy. Just before the mountains. Do you remember what the mountains are called?'

'Dol-o-mites,' intoned Joey.

'Quite right. Clever boy,' approved Rafaello.

He went on chatting as he made his way on to the autostrada heading towards the north of Italy. Unlike the grim duty visit to his father in Amalfi, this time he was looking forward to a long weekend away.

He addressed Alaina, sitting beside Joey as she always did when they travelled long distance with him, in order to be on hand for toys, audio books, drinks from his no-spill beaker, fortifying snacks and being on hand in general.

'I hope you get on with Dante—he and I go back a long way. And, as you know, his wife is English too.'

'And their little boy is around eighteen months, I think you said?'

'Thereabouts. I'm his godfather, so I should know. But,

well...' Rafaello gave something of a shrug 'I wasn't really into babies when he was born. Luckily, Dante is totally besotted—as is Connie.' He sounded amused.

'I'm looking forward to meeting them all,' said Alaina.

'You'll like Connie—it's impossible not to. She has a very sweet nature. It's a shame they live so far away. But Dante's work keeps him in Milan—he's in finance. Connie's a stay-at-home mum, like you.'

He gained the autostrada, settling into a steady pace that ate up the miles. The scenery became more dramatic as they edged along the Apennines, and he went back to telling Joey about the regions they were passing through. They stopped for lunch off the autostrada, then resumed their drive.

By the time they reached the lush, flat landscape of Lombardy Joey had dozed off, but he surfaced, refreshed, as Rafaello turned into the drive of Dante's villa. He was glad to visit his old friend. Although conscious, all the same, of a sense of irony that he would be turning up with not only a wife but a four-year-old in tow.

Dante had already ragged him about it over the phone, and Rafaello knew, resignedly, that he would be on the receiving end of his friend's open amusement at this abrupt change in Rafaello's lifestyle in person.

And so it proved.

'Raf—the married man and fond *papà*! Who'd have thought?' Dante greeted him, slapping him heartily on the shoulder as they all disembarked from the car.

His wife's greeting was less teasing. 'Raf, how lovely to see you again—it's been far too long! I'm dying to meet Alaina—and the gorgeous, *gorgeous* Joey!'

Connie kissed him on the cheek, but her attention was

on Alaina, now extricating Joey from his child seat. Rafaello watched Dante's wife smile warmly at her.

'Welcome, welcome! And this is Joey—oh, you are just *so* adorable!'

Joey was clambering down, looking interestedly around him. Alaina was returning Connie's greetings, and Dante came up to her, holding out his hand.

'Alaina—good to meet you.'

Rafaello could see Dante's eyes alive with interest in the woman he had married.

'Come on in. I can see that you don't manage to travel any more lightly than Connie and I do!' His voice was amused. 'It's amazing just how much stuff a baby needs—and it looks like it just increases as they get older!' He turned his attention to Joey. 'Hello, young man—I'm Dante. This is Connie. Come inside and meet Benito. He's younger than you, so you'll have to be gentle with him.'

They all made their way indoors, with Dante leading them through the villa out into the garden beyond.

'A pool!' Joey exclaimed happily. His contentment was guaranteed, and he ran forward eagerly. 'Can we swim now?' he asked.

'In a while,' Dante told him. 'Time for cake first.'

This was a sufficient diversion for Joey, and he quickly settled himself at the wooden table set out under a wide awning. Connie had re-emerged from the house, holding the hand of an infant who was wobbling forward.

Now it was Alaina's turn to exclaim.

'Oh, but you are just *darling*!' she enthused.

Lifting Benito into his highchair, Connie beamed. Rafaello watched as she and Alaina settled into mum-talk and turned to Dante.

'OK, get it out of your system,' he said dryly. 'The obvious hilarity of my finding myself a ready-made father and taking a ready-made wife…'

Dante's dark eyes glinted with appreciative humour. But it was not solely directed at Rafaello. 'I'm hardly one to talk, Raf—Connie was a gift I never saw coming too. And it looks like you've struck just as lucky with Alaina.'

He laid an arm around Rafaello's shoulder, but it was a comradely one.

'Tell me all about it later, when the girls are cosying up. It will be nice for Connie to speak English. I hope they get on…'

'No one could fail to get on with Connie,' Rafaello said.

They laughed, sitting themselves down as a maid came out of the house bearing a large tray of tea things.

Connie turned to Alaina. 'I'm so glad you're here—I've baked a Victoria sponge for us, and chocolate fairy cakes for the infantry. Do you drink tea, or have you converted to coffee completely?'

'Tea would be lovely, thank you,' Alaina was answering. 'I can't cope with *espresso*, though I love *cappuccino*. Rafaello has a fearsome machine in the kitchen, but I'm terrified of using it. I leave it to our wonderful housekeeper, Maria. But mostly I drink tea. It never quite tastes the same, though, even with imported tea.'

'It's the water,' Connie was saying. 'Or the British weather! Or something. Yes, Benito…' she turned her attention to her son '…choccy cake *is* coming. I promise. But guests first. Now, Joey, would you like a fairy cake with a flaky chocolate bar in the icing, or one with chocolate buttons?'

'Both!' announced Joey happily.

It was not long before a substantial amount of chocolate icing had transferred itself to both Joey and Benito, and the atmosphere had settled into one of complete conviviality. Rafaello could see that Alaina was hitting it off with Connie, chatting away in English, while he and Dante lapsed into Italian for a casual catch up.

After tea, as promised, a swimming session beckoned. Rafaello saw his friend's eyes soften and linger on Connie's lush figure as she stood in her one-piece swimsuit, a wriggling Benito in her arms.

Dante caught Rafaello's eye. 'Every day I give thanks for her!' he said, his voice heartfelt. Then his expression changed. 'And you, old friend, do you give such thanks?'

A real question was there in his tone, however lightly spoken. Rafaello did not quite meet his eyes, looking back, instead, to where Joey was now vigorously splashing away, batting himself forward on his water wings. Alaina was gracefully swimming alongside him.

'I give thanks that I found my son,' he said.

He was aware that Dante was still looking at him, but did not turn his head to face him.

'Why did Alaina not tell you that she was pregnant?'

Dante's voice was neutral. But Rafaello knew perfectly well the question wasn't neutral at all.

He was silent for a moment, then spoke carefully.

'We had an affair, Dante. That was all. I made it clear that was all it could be when I became aware, I acknowledge, that she might have liked…something more. But I was flying back to Italy…she was working out there in the Caribbean. And I— Well, as you know, I was perfectly happy with the way I lived my life.'

'Avoiding commitment,' Dante said dryly.

Rafaello's eyebrows rose, and now he did glance at his friend. 'As you did—before Connie.'

'For very different reasons, Raf,' Dante replied. 'I'd

never had time to commit—nor met anyone I wanted to commit to.'

'The second reason I share with you,' Rafaello answered.

'And now?' Dante's voice was probing, his own eyebrow raised questioningly.

Rafaello looked away again. Dante was too old a friend to prevaricate with. So he spoke the truth. Blunt, but honest.

'My commitment is not of my own making. The situation is as it is and I accept it. Joey is my son. I have a lifelong responsibility for him and to him. He comes with Alaina. And Alaina,' he said, 'comes with very significant...compensations.' His gaze went back to Dante. 'She and I get on perfectly well. She, like me, has accepted the necessity of our current situation and has adapted to it. I treat her, I hope, with respect and consideration. We are making a good home for Joey, and that is our priority. As for ourselves... Well, the compensations are, as I say—and as is obvious—' his glance now was pointed '—significant.'

Dante held his gaze. 'But you would not have chosen this of your own free will—compensations or not? Is that really what you're saying?'

The question hung in the air. Rafaello wished Dante had not asked it. Because the answer was irrelevant.

His own words just now to Dante echoed in his head. *'The situation is as it is and I accept it.'*

That was the only answer to be given.

Whatever else it was that Dante was probing for...

How can he understand my situation? The arrival, out of the blue, of a ready-made son I had never envisaged? The necessary and completely essential reaction I had to

give to that? Neither I nor Alaina had any say in what that
reaction had to be—we simply had to accept it and adapt
our lives accordingly. For Joey's sake. And we have. We
have done just that.

Dante's questioning eyes were still on him. Rafaello
wanted him to back off.

Then Connie's voice pierced the moment, and he was
glad.

'Dante! Can you throw in that inflatable for Joey?'
she called from the water. 'It's just over there by the pool
house.'

Rafaello welcomed the diversion. Dante was probing
where it was pointless to go. He got to his feet along with
his friend. Time to join the pool party. Not to think about
things that had no purpose, no place in the life he now led.

Had no choice but to lead.

The long weekend passed very enjoyably. Dante and Connie were the most welcoming and hospitable of hosts, and
just as Dante and Rafaello relaxed back into what was
clearly, Alaina could see, a long-standing friendship, so
a new friendship was being forged between herself and
Dante's wife.

As Rafaello and Dante, helped by Joey, packed up
the car, ready for them to set off back to Rome, Connie
warmly invited them to come again.

'Or you come to us,' Alaina returned smilingly.
'Though I know that travelling with a little one is less
easy than it is with Joey.'

'I'm sure we'll manage something between us.' Connie
smiled. 'And as the boys get older it will become easier.
Unless, of course, we start all over again with another

sproglet. Dante and I are keen, but these things are never certain. What about you and Raf?' she asked.

Alaina was silent for a moment. Then, slowly, she spoke. 'Rafaello and I aren't a...a normal family, Connie. When I had Joey I never expected Rafaello to play any part in his upbringing—in his life, really.'

Connie was staring at her, a frown on her face. 'But why?' She took a breath. 'I'm being tactless, and I'm sorry, but it seems so strange to me not to tell a child's father that he is one!'

Again Alaina was silent for a moment before she answered, and she knew she spoke hesitantly.

'I just didn't think he'd welcome the news. We...we only had a holiday romance, Connie. It was all very magical and glamorous—romancing under the tropical moon and all that stuff!—and Rafaello...' she made a face '...he's a pretty hard guy to resist. And, to be honest, I didn't want to resist him at all.'

'Not many women do,' said Connie dryly. 'He's quite different from Dante in his appeal, but I know he's got it in spades! Even I could see that when I met him—and I was totally besotted with Dante! Raf is Mr Cool personified. He...' she frowned '...plays the field. Well,' she amended, 'he used to—'

'That,' said Alaina, 'I can well believe. And it only lends weight to my argument. I didn't think he'd welcome discovering that one of his passing romances was pregnant. I didn't think it fair to burden him with it. I don't need financial support, and there are plenty of other single mums around. And also—'

She broke off, took a breath, and looked Connie straight in the eye.

'Also, I didn't want Joey having anything to do with a

father who would have preferred he didn't exist. *No* child should grow up knowing that!'

Now Connie was staring at Alaina with concern in her expression.

Alaina gave a half-shrug. 'My father made it pretty obvious he had no interest in me. He found it hard, if not impossible, to be affectionate. If he didn't exactly resent my existence, he certainly didn't take much interest in it. So...' she took another breath '... I didn't want to risk that for Joey.'

'But Raf's so *good* with Joey!' Connie protested.

'Yes,' said Alaina, 'he is. But he might not have been.'

He might have been like his own icy, condemning father, as well as like mine.

The thought was chilling.

'And Joey clearly gets on like a house on fire with Raf!' Connie continued.

Alaina's expression softened. 'Joey's accepted him in his life and I'm so very glad of that. He's adapted incredibly well to coming out to Italy, to the new life we lead now.'

Connie looked at her, another question in her eyes. 'And what about you? Have you adapted well?' She paused. 'It must have been a big thing,' she said quietly, 'giving up the life you'd made for yourself and Joey and moving out here. And, of course, marrying Rafaello.'

'Yes, it was,' Alaina replied. She kept her voice measured. 'But it had to be done. Rafaello had to do it and so did I. I hadn't planned it—but once he'd declared he wanted to be in Joey's life permanently there really wasn't an alternative. As for adapting to it...well, I suppose I have.'

She dropped her gaze, aware that Connie was still look-ing at her.

'And are you happy?' she asked.

Alaina could feel her heart beating. Did it seem louder than it should be? And if it did, why should that be?

'I'm as happy as the situation permits,' she said care-fully. She turned back to Connie and met her gaze full-on. 'I have so much, Connie! I have Joey… I have an easy, luxurious life! I live in a beautiful villa just outside Rome. I have staff to run it and I have a glittering social life as well, with fabulous gowns and jewels! I have a husband who is attentive and considerate, who has taken Joey into his life, and I can't fault his treatment of him! And I can't fault Rafaello's attentions to me either!'

She coloured slightly, but went on, woman-to-woman—both of them, after all, were married to men any other woman would envy them for as far as sexual attractive-ness was concerned, let alone the wealth and glamour that went with them.

'He's made it crystal-clear that whatever flared be-tween us five years ago is still there, and that there's no point denying it or quenching it. So…so we don't. And… and that's very good. I mean…' She coloured again, giv-ing a half-laugh. 'Well, I'm sure you know what I mean! You don't need diagrams! Rafaello is incredibly attractive, and I'm no more able to resist his Mr Cool charm now than I was five years ago. And there's no need for me to do so anyway. In fact…' she drew a breath '…our mar-riage probably wouldn't work without it, I can be honest enough to admit that.'

She dropped her gaze again, still feeling that stronger heartbeat inside her. This was a strange conversation to be having—and had Connie not been the wife of Rafaello's closest friend she'd never have had it. Certainly not, she realised, with any of the new mothers she'd been meeting as she settled into her new life.

She realised Connie was starting to speak again, and heard the careful question in her voice.

'And is that enough?' she asked.

The thudding in Alaina's heart was louder than ever. Her voice was thin as she eventually answered.

'I don't know,' she said.

But even as she spoke she felt that dangerously thin ice beneath her crack and fracture.

She looked away, the answer she'd given Connie echoing in her head.

I don't know.

But she did know. Yet she dared not say it. Dared not admit it or the carefully constructed life she'd made for herself and Joey out here in Italy would plunge through that dangerously thin ice...

Taking her with it.

Rafaello depressed the accelerator and the car shot forward along the autostrada. He had enjoyed their stay with Dante and Connie—impossible not to, given his long friendship with Dante and his fondness for Connie. Yet it had disturbed him too.

Dante had talked to him openly about the marriage he'd made with Alaina for Joey's sake, and Rafaello had answered as openly. Yet he'd felt an unspoken criticism—a challenge—coming from Dante. His mouth tightened. Dante had an idyllic marriage—what could he know of how it was between himself and Alaina?

On the surface, Dante and Connie and their little boy were identical to himself, Alaina and Joey, apart from Benito's younger age. But there was a difference all the same.

His friends had chosen the life they were leading.

I didn't. It was imposed on me. And however much I enjoy the...compensations it affords me, nothing gets away from that blunt truth. I didn't choose the life I now lead.

In his head he heard again the question Dante had put to him. Asking him bluntly whether he would have chosen the life he was leading now of his own free will.

It was a question he never allowed himself to ask. Because there was no purpose in asking. It was hypothetical...irrelevant.

His glance went to the rear-view mirror. He could see Alaina, quietly reading to Joey one of his favourite train stories. She seemed subdued, he fancied. Did she, too, feel the difference between themselves and Dante and Connie?

But what did it matter if she did? There was no more point in asking her the question Dante had put to him than it had been to ask it of himself.

She accepts the situation...as do I. What else can we do?

Thoughts moved across his mind. Was this how his father had felt when he'd realised how completely ill-matched to each other he and the woman he'd married were? Yet he'd accepted the situation.

But their marriage was a disaster!

His and Alaina's was nothing like that. He was nothing like his father, and Alaina was nothing like his mother. There was no comparison—none. He was not cold or resentful, as his father had been, and Alaina was not needy and clinging as his mother had been.

We are fine as we are—as fine as we need to be.

And that, in the end, was all that could be said. All that could be done.

And yet his hands tightened over the wheel and his expression, as he accelerated again to overtake another car, was set.

CHAPTER THIRTEEN

ALAINA WAS STUDYING the calendar. In little more than a month Joey would be starting school. The summer had flashed by. She frowned. How had that happened so quickly?

She felt her thoughts go off at a tangent. With Joey at school every day, she'd need to find something for herself to do. Maria and Giorgio ran the villa perfectly, so maybe she could get a job of some kind? She wasn't sure what—this wasn't a touristy part of Italy, and hospitality was really all she knew. It would need to be something that could be worked around Joey's school timetable, of course, and his school holidays. And around any socialising Rafaello wanted her to share in.

Speaking of which, there was a fancy bash coming up this very weekend—some glittering charity gala in Rome, for which she would need to look her very best. She had a hair appointment booked already, plus an appointment for getting her nails done too, and a facial. All would be needed for her to be Signora Ranieri, doing her husband proud.

Her mind ran on to which evening gown would suit—her wardrobe now held plenty to choose from—and what jewels would best go with it. Rafaello had presented her with additions to the diamond necklace, and her jewellery case now held sapphires, rubies and emeralds, as well as some very beautiful pearls.

Not that she considered any of them *hers*. They were Rafaello's, and she merely wore them as his wife. The same was true of the exorbitantly expensive designer evening gowns she wore the jewellery with. The same was true of her whole lifestyle out here, really...

The lifestyle that came courtesy of Joey.

Deliberately, she changed her expression. She hadn't asked for this lavish lifestyle—and she hadn't asked or expected Rafaello to provide it.

Or even to marry me.

Thoughts flickered in her head. She'd have been perfectly happy staying in England, continuing to work as she had, juggling her career with motherhood. Rafaello might have simply been a regular visitor, or she might have gone for part time working, maybe, and brought Joey out here for regular visits. As Joey had grown up he would have spent time on his own with Rafaello, if that was what they'd both wanted. These days parents did not always live together, and their children were none the worse for it. It could work flexibly and very well. Her friend Ryan managed being a divorced dad perfectly, after all.

She headed towards the kitchen, where Maria was showing Joey how to make fresh ravioli, wanting to put such thoughts out of her head. This was the life she led and that was all there was to it. No point thinking about anything else.

No point remembering that weekend with Dante and Connie. Seeing them together with their little boy. A truly happy family. An adored baby, and parents who adored each other too...

A pang struck her, like an ache in her side. She banished that too, for there was no point feeling it. Dante and Connie were lucky—so lucky. They loved each other, were made for each other. She was not jealous of them... only envious...

No, don't go there! Theirs is a marriage based on love—a normal marriage! They were married and then they started a family...the normal order of things. For Rafaello and me it was not like that.

She shut her eyes for a moment. Hearing the words in her head. Tolling like a bell she could not silence.

Nor can it ever be like that.

She pushed the kitchen door open.

'Mummy, come and see!'

Joey's voice was gleeful as Alaina went into the kitchen. He was kneeling on a chair at the long, scrubbed wooden kitchen table, diligently working away under Maria's supervision. Dutifully she admired the somewhat ragged-looking, zig-zag-edged pasta squares that Joey was busy cutting with a zig-zag roller.

'I hope those are for our lunch,' she said, and smiled.

'He is learning very fast!' Maria beamed.

'You're an excellent teacher,' Alaina complimented her. 'And thank you for looking after him this weekend while I'm in the city. All next week, I know, you and Giorgio are off to visit your son and daughter-in-law in Puglia. I haven't forgotten. It's a well-deserved break for you both!' she assured Maria.

They discussed practicalities for a few moments, then Alaina left them to it. A restlessness filled her, and she didn't know why. Nothing had changed, after all, had it?

She halted in her tracks.

Maybe that was the problem. Nothing *had* changed.

Her life here was flowing smoothly and would go on doing so. What had she to complain about? Yet into her head came the question Connie had put to her as she'd outlined her smooth, untroubled life, her *dolce vita* here with Joey and Rafaello.

'And is that enough?'

She heard her own answer echo.

'I don't know.'

It hung there again, in her head. And beneath her feet the smooth thin ice of her smoothly flowing life once again seemed to be suddenly dangerously thinner.

The charity gala was a glittering affair indeed, held at one of the huge aristocratic Renaissance *palazzos* in Rome. Alaina looked stunning, she knew, in an off-the-shoulder gown in lemon glacé satin and a pearl choker, her hair swept up into an elaborate style, with drop pearl earrings and pearl combs completing the extravagant look. At her side Rafaello, in white tie, looked as knock-out as he always did.

Compliments came their way, with appreciative looks from females at Rafaello and from males at herself. Conversation was easy, many faces familiar now, and the evening was sumptuous.

When they returned to Rafaello's apartment he undressed her slowly, sensually, and then just as slowly and sensually made love to her in a way that reduced her body to molten lava…

Over a late, leisurely breakfast, Rafaello poured himself some coffee.

'I'm afraid I won't be coming back with you to the villa today,' he told her. 'A business trip's come up at short notice and I have to fly out first thing.'

'Where this time?' Alaina asked conversationally.

'Long haul, alas...'

There was a slight air of hesitancy about him that she picked up on. It was explained as he went on.

'The Caribbean. The same client that called me over there five years ago. He's getting divorced again. From the woman he'd left his then wife for when I handled the divorce for him that time.'

The cynical note was there in his voice quite openly—Alaina could hear it. But it was not that that she paid attention to.

A ripple of something she could not name had gone through her.

'Will...will you be away long?'

He took a mouthful of his coffee and shrugged. 'I hope not, but he's a difficult character. He'll want to dispose of this wife as cheaply as he can.'

Alaina looked at him. 'So few of your clients seem like very agreeable people,' she said.

His mouth twisted. 'They're the ones I charge the highest fees for.'

She let that pass. What did she care about clients who didn't like paying their taxes, or liked to divorce their wives on the cheap? But he was speaking again, and she made herself listen, wondering why it was so disquieting to think of Rafaello going out to the island where they had first met. What had happened there had led directly to her sitting here having breakfast with him at his opulent Rome apartment, sharing his life.

'I was wondering...' he was saying, and she heard uncertainty in his voice, which was unusual for him. 'Whether you might like to join me once I'm done with work there. Have a holiday out there.'

She looked at him. 'Joey's too young for a long-haul flight,' she said.

'I was thinking of just you,' he replied. He looked at her. 'For old times' sake, perhaps.' His voice was light. Dispassionate. As if he were feeling his way...

She swallowed. 'I wouldn't like to leave Joey and be so far away. And besides, Maria and Giorgio are away all next week, visiting their son in Puglia. I can't ask them to change their plans...it wouldn't be fair.'

He gave a slight shrug, as though it were of no importance. Reached for his coffee cup again.

She heard herself continue, wondering why she did, and whether it was wise to do so.

'And besides, maybe...maybe it wouldn't be a good idea, Rafaello. Maybe it's best to leave the past alone.'

She looked away for a moment, blinking. In her mind's eye she was under that hotel portico, watching Rafaello drive away from her.

She felt the same pang that had smitten her when she'd compared Dante and Connie's loving marriage to her own with Rafaello.

Five years ago she had watched Rafaello leave her life. Watched and known with quelling awareness just how very close she had come to stepping off the brink of that dangerous cliff her mother had warned her about her all her life. She had almost stepped off and plunged down, down, down... Into a love that could never be returned. Never be requited. Never be shared with the one person she most longed to share it...

I stepped back then—I managed to do it. Managed to save myself from my mother's fate.

Rafaello was changing the subject, making some innocuous remark about the charity gala the night before.

Alaina pulled herself together, made some appropriate reply.

She got through the rest of breakfast. Then, getting to her feet, she said, her manner unchanged, 'Why don't I head back to the villa now? I'm sure you'll be prepping for whatever will be required of you next week with your client, and you'll want to pack and so forth. Maria and Giorgio will want to pack too, I expect, so I'll take over on the Joey front this afternoon.'

'I can drive you back—' Rafaello began, but she shook her head.

'No, stay here—Joey will be disappointed if he gets to see you and then you disappear again. If your driver is off duty I'll just take a taxi to the villa.'

Which was what she did.

As she took her leave of Rafaello she kissed him goodbye, as she always did when they separated. Her kiss was light, her manner as it always was with him. As was his with her. He saw her into the taxi, lifted a hand in casual farewell as it moved off.

He did not see—could not see—that Alaina had sat back, tilted back her head, and that in her face was a look that had not been there for a long time. For five long years…

On Monday morning she saw Maria and Giorgio off, with Joey waving manically to them as they drove away. Then, slowly, she went back indoors. The same restlessness that had assailed her before the weekend came again. Plucking at her…disquieting her.

On sudden impulse she stooped down, catching Joey.

'Joey, munchkin—Papà is away, and Maria and Giorgio have gone away, so why don't we…?' She took a breath.

'Why don't we do the same? Let's have an adventure of our own—a little holiday! Let's go and see...' She swallowed, but then she said it. 'Our old home.'

Joey looked at her. 'Is it still there?'

She nodded. 'Yes,' she said slowly, 'it's still there.'

By the end of the day she was letting herself into her little house in England, wondering if she had just made the worst decision of her life or the only one she could make.

The only one that would not destroy her utterly.

Rafaello stood out on the balcony of his hotel room, resting his hand lightly on the balustrade. The t air was warm, much warmer than at home, and he could hear the soft lapping of the sea on the beach beyond the lush gardens. The noise of tree frogs chirruping unseen in the palm trees made a different chorus from that of the cicadas he was used to. Above the azure sea the sun was a blaze of gold.

Memory shafted through him. A memory of standing like this, but with Alaina at his side. The Alaina of five years ago. The Alaina he had seen, desired, and seduced so very pleasurably. And it had been completely mutual.

Mutual right up until the end.

His expression changed, and he frowned. It was not his fault he had not wanted what she had wanted. Nor her fault that she had. They had simply wanted different things, that was all.

I wanted the life I'd always led and saw no reason for anything different.

Joey's existence had changed all that for ever.

What if I still didn't know Joey existed?

Images crowded into his mind. Joey splashing in the swimming pool. Joey running around the garden. Joey sitting in his car seat, asking him questions. Joey playing with his building bricks and toy trains. Joey drowsing against him as he read him his bedtime story...

Abruptly, suddenly wanting to hear Joey's piping voice, he reached for his phone. The time difference was such that it was already the evening in Italy. He phoned Alaina's mobile, but it went to voicemail. Probably she was getting Joey to bed already. He would have to trt again in the morning.

He set down his phone, conscious of a feeling of disappointment that he hadn't been able to speak to Joey, and stood looking out over the lush gardens of the Falcone again, palm trees waving in the warm breeze.

And it was not only Joey's voice he wanted to hear. It was a shame Alaina would not be joining him. It would have been good to see her here again. Recapturing what they had once had.

But we had only a brief romance—nothing more than that.

And what was the use of seeking to recapture something so brief?

He abandoned his thoughts, heading down to the dining room to enjoy the Falcone's celebrated cuisine.

Tomorrow he had to face his difficult client. Alaina's words over breakfast the day before echoed in his head. Found resonance. Why did he bother with clients like this one, whose treatment of women was shameful, however well he paid his lawyer to dispose of them? Or the Geneva-based client reluctant to spend any of his vast wealth on paying the taxes he owed? Or any similar unscrupulous if lucrative clients?

Maybe he should prune his client list when he got back to Rome. Get rid of such clients, however much revenue they brought in. His father would not approve—but then his father wasn't running the firm any more.

But it was best not to think of his father. He had heard nothing from him since their brief duty visit earlier that summer. As predicted, his father had taken not the slightest interest in his grandson.

His thoughts flickered. Had it been his mother who was still alive…

No, best not to think of his mother either. Besides being all over Joey, she would have woven ludicrous, unreal dreams around the marriage he had made, never accepting that his marriage to Alaina was the way it was for the reason it was. Nothing more than that.

'Signor Ranieri, how good to have you with us again!'

The maître d' was greeting him fulsomely, exhibiting the Falcone's reputation for faultless service in remembering a guest who had not visited for five years, dispelling pointless thoughts about what his mother would have wanted his marriage to be—when it was simply not.

He took his place at the table he was ushered to, memory flickering yet again. He'd brought Alaina to dine here and she'd sat gazing at him, her eyes alight, blazing with all that she had never hidden. All that she had offered.

But he had taken only what he'd wanted to take then. Wanting no more of her than that.

And nothing has changed.

Neither the five years between, nor Joey's existence, nor their marriage, made any difference to that.

It's all I want of her—what I had then, and what I have now.

Nothing else.

Alaina heard her phone ping. She ignored it. It would be Rafaello again. The call had gone to voicemail, but she hadn't played it back yet. Her thoughts were too troubled to do so. Joey was in bed, in his old bedroom, tired after the journey from Rome and disorientated too.

She too was disorientated—how could it be otherwise? It felt so strange to be back in the UK, and had felt even stranger to climb out of their taxi from the airport and go into the little house that had once been her home. For Joey's sake, though, she had to hold it together, however strange she felt. And however tight her insides were at the thought of the step she'd taken so precipitately.

I'm not thinking about it—not yet. I can't. I'll think about it later.

But when later came—with Joey safely asleep, clutching his teddy—and she had had a sketchy supper of tinned soup and unpacked their suitcase, she was lying in her old, familiar and yet now so strange bed, the thoughts came anyway.

Difficult, confusing, painful thoughts, that went round and round in her stubbornly sleepless head.

Thoughts she didn't want to think—didn't want to face. Thoughts she didn't want stirring up emotions she didn't want either.

Though she finally fell asleep, it was not a peaceful, restorative sleep, and when in the early hours she heard Joey cry out, calling plaintively for her, she went into his room, getting into bed with him and hugging him, holding him close until he fell asleep again, reassured by her presence in what had become an alien place for him.

And yet again the question circled in her head.

Have I done the right thing or the wrong thing? The right thing or the wrong thing?

And right—or wrong—for who?

For her—or for Joey?

Because if it's only for me, then I shouldn't do it.

She gazed blankly at the ceiling as daylight crept into the room through the drawn curtains.

But at what cost to me?

And that, she knew, was the hardest question of all to ask. Let alone answer…

Rafaello was reading Alaina's text. It was the only communication he'd had from her since leaving Italy. She hadn't returned his calls. Was it just the time difference being awkward?

But as he read her text, his brows snapping into a frown, he realised that it was nothing to do with the time difference. He stared down at the phone in his hand. Her text incised itself upon him.

She had gone to England. Taking Joey with her. She'd given no explanation, and certainly no indication of how long she would be there.

His frown deepened.

Slowly, he texted back.

What brought this on?

No answer came.

He slid his phone away. He had to go and meet his client at the appointed hour this morning. He would do that, then try and get hold of Alaina.

But his calls went to voicemail and she did not phone back or text again.

By the evening he had made his mind up. He phoned his client, cancelled their next meeting, ignored the angry protestations heaped upon him, and booked the first flight off the island.

What the hell is going on?
The question circled. Unanswerable and unanswered.

Alaina could hear the sound of a raucous cartoon playing
on the TV in the living room, keeping Joey entertained.
She was standing in the kitchen, holding her phone. There
were more texts from Rafaello, more voicemails. Sounding more frustrated, increasingly terse. She had to answer…find something she could say.

Carefully, she texted him.

I wanted to check on my house. This seemed like a good
time, with you away all week.

His reply came immediately.

When are you back? I'm in Rome. I have cut short my
time in the Caribbean.

She stared at the screen, knowing her heart rate was
thudding. Why had he cut his trip short? Because she'd
said she wasn't in Italy?

She texted back:

Not sure.

Again, his reply came instantly.

Tell me when you are.

She turned her phone off. She didn't want him phon-
ing her. Could not cope with it. Could cope with nothing
right now—not even Joey.

She could cope with nothing at all. Least of all the knowledge of what she had done.

Or why.

Rafaello lay in his bed at his apartment. It was impossible to sleep, and jet lag had nothing to do with it. He was just lying there, staring blankly at the darkened ceiling. The bed was too large, and he was alone in it.

But he often slept alone when he was in the apartment without Alaina during the working week, so why, now, did it feel so…?

So wrong.

It was a question he could not answer. But there were a whole stack of questions piling up that he could not answer.

Only Alaina could.

And she was not giving any answers. None that made sense.

He lay, staring unseeing into the dark. Conscious that his heart rate was elevated, tension netting him. What was Alaina playing at—and why?

And why, above all, was there a churning in his guts that should not be there. Should not be there at all…

Joey was fretful. His initial excitement at being back in the house he'd once lived in had dissipated. He was finding fault with it. His toys were all in Italy and there was no swimming pool. Nor was there Maria and Giorgio.

And he wanted his *papà*.

'Papà is away on business,' Alaina told him evasively. She put a smile on her face. 'I'm going to see whether we can visit Betsy. That would be nice!'

But on texting Ryan to tell him they were unexpectedly back in the UK she learnt that Betsy was off with her mother on holiday.

Ryan phoned her. 'How come you're back?' he asked. 'Is it just a flying visit?'

'I'm not sure,' Alaina replied, conscious of Joey nearby, discontentedly watching TV.

Alaina took the phone into the kitchen, not sure what to tell Ryan.

Because I'm not sure of anything.

But that wasn't true, and she knew it. She was sure of something. Something that was starting to feel like concrete, setting in a lump within her, heavy and hard.

She heard only silence from Ryan. Then, 'Alaina, is everything all right? I mean, with…with you and Rafaello?'

The silence now came from Alaina. Then, 'I'm leaving him, Ryan.'

She had said it. The words she had been trying not to say. The words she had been silencing all the way from Italy. The words which now, like that concrete setting inside her, were the hardest and heaviest she had ever had to speak.

I'm leaving him…

CHAPTER FOURTEEN

'RAF—GOOD TO see you.'

Dante settled himself down at the table in the restaurant where Rafaello, with extreme reluctance, had agreed to meet him for lunch during his friend's impromptu business trip to Rome.

The timing could not have been worse.

He let Dante order martinis for both of them.

'How's things? The *bellissima* Alaina and the cherubic Joey?'

'They're in the UK,' Rafaello answered. He was aware his voice was light...deliberately so.

'Oh, shame. I'm under instructions from Connie to visit while I'm here and report back.'

'Report back on what?' Rafaello's voice had sharpened, and he set his water glass on the table with a click.

Dante stared. 'Just how they're doing—how you're all doing.' He leant forward a fraction, his expression changing. 'Raf...?'

Rafaello sat back. Tension had formed across his shoulders. To others he might seem to withdraw behind his customary cool demeanour, holding the world at bay, immune behind his honed-to-perfection guard—the guard that enabled him to lead the life he liked to lead, staying observant, amused, sardonic, distanced from any personal involvement—but Dante knew him better than any other person in his life.

And he knew Dante. Knew that Dante took life by the shoulders and shook it till it did what he wanted of it. Rafaello took a far less combative stance, stepping with faultless precision along the path of life even when that path had to be altered and rerouted in directions he had never envisaged in the light of completely unforeseeable circumstances.

Like the discovery that he had a son.

And his making a wife of the woman who'd borne him.

'Raf?' Dante prompted again.

The waiter placed their martinis in front of them and took himself off. Dante ignored his martini, still eyeballing Rafaello.

'OK, what's up?' he said abruptly. 'And don't brush me off, Raf. This is me, Dante, remember? I don't take brush-offs.' He took a breath. 'So…?'

Rafaello's focus slid past him. For a moment he did not answer. Could not. Then his eyes went back to Dante, meeting his bullishly insistent gaze straight on.

'Alaina wants a divorce,' he said bluntly.

'Divorce?' Ryan's voice was openly shocked. 'Good God, *why*? I thought it had all worked out OK with Rafaello.'

Ryan had turned up after work and was now sitting in Alaina's tiny garden. Joey was still parked in front of the TV, though Alaina felt bad about it. Tomorrow they must go and replenish his empty toybox and bookshelf. And she'd have to contact the school he'd been going to go to here in the autumn, and hope they still had a place for him. Then she needed to see if the hotel would take her back.

Restart my life.

Her eyes went to her old friend, saw the shock open on his face as well as hearing it in his voice. She swallowed. It was like swallowing concrete.

'I thought I could do it…being married to him like that,' she said. 'But I didn't… I didn't think it through.'

She went silent, dropping her gaze away from Ryan.

He waited a moment, then spoke, his voice both careful, and gentle. 'So…what went wrong?' he asked.

Alaina lifted her eyes to him. Her throat had closed. In a voice that was almost impossible to get out, she told him…

Rafaello was at the villa. He'd gone there deliberately, immediately after his lunch with Dante. Maria and Giorgio were still away, and the emptiness of the place echoed all around him.

No piping sound of Joey's voice greeting him. No Joey running up to him and hugging him, waiting for him to stoop down and scoop him up, return the hug…

No Alaina's voice to break the echoing silence, welcoming him home…

Only the echo of Dante's voice in his head. Challenging. Demanding.

So, what are you going to do?

He heard his own answer, given in his cool, contained voice:

I'm considering my options.

Dante had glowered at him.

'This is not one of your damn clients you're talking about! This, Raf, is your wife and your son.'

Rafaello had looked at him.

'You mistake the situation. It is my son and his mother.'

Dante's eyes had narrowed.

'Is that so?' he'd asked.

Rafaello had met the narrowed gaze full-on.

'Yes,' he'd answered coolly. *'Alaina is my wife only because she is the mother of my son.'*

Now, as he stood out on the terrace in the dusk, the noise of the cicadas was incessant in the vegetation beyond the pool. The pool lights were turning the water to glowing iridescence, a moth was fluttering nearby, and the scent of honeysuckle caught at him from where it clambered up a trellis.

He heard Dante's taunting question again.

'Is that so?'

He stared at the emptiness ahead of him. The emptiness all around him. The emptiness inside him. The emptiness that was echoing with thoughts he did not want to think. About someone he did not want to think about.

Alaina.

The mother of his son. The son she had not told him about because she had known he would not welcome the news or the responsibility it would impose upon him. The responsibility he had now taken on—that had made him change his life completely, made him take Alaina as his wife…take her to bed…take only what he'd wanted of her before, all those years ago in the Caribbean. Then in an affair—only that. But now in a marriage…because of Joey.

I married her because it kept things simple. It gave me Joey without a fight, and it made creating a home for him straightforward. It regularised things. Legitimated them. Normalised them. Mother, father, child.

A family unit.

Except family units were made after marriage, not before. Before family units came husband and wife. That was what came first.

You choose your spouse and then, and only then, do you start a family. When you know your choice of spouse was right.

His mouth twisted painfully. Half his clients never chose right…

Nor had his parents.

Theirs had been a disastrous marriage from the start. But they'd had a son, all the same. A son who had grown up witnessing the non-stop car crash that his parents' marriage had been. A son who had found the self-protection he needed by emotionally withdrawing from it all.

It was a self-protection he still relied on implicitly. It served him well. Always had.

Until now.

His gaze went out over the empty pool, then back to the empty house. No Joey tucked up in bed, falling asleep as his bedtime story finished, his dark eyes closing in drowsy slumber as Rafaello smoothed his hair and left the room on quiet feet. No Alaina curled up on the sofa sipping her white wine, leafing through a glossy magazine. Lifting her lovely eyes to look at him. Smiling up at him…

And suddenly, out of nowhere, a knife plunged into his side. Vicious…brutal. Striking into his ribs, his lungs, cutting off his breath. It was a pain like nothing he had ever felt. Ever allowed himself to feel.

But now it skewered him.

He shut his eyes, unable to bear it.

Alaina let Joey scramble out of the car seat in her little car, then headed for the front door. They'd been shopping, including buying some toys and books, but Joey's mood was

still subdued. He'd asked when they were going home…
Alaina had been evasive.

Anxiety and so much more plucked at her. Had it been
rash to tell Rafaello by text that she wanted a divorce?
But how could she possibly speak to him? And her position now, surely, was stronger than it had been when he'd
first talked about custody battles. She was his legal wife,
and even with the prenup she'd signed surely that would
mean she could afford a lawyer as tough as him?

But would it really come to that? Please, God, no…
Could they not just work out something that would give
her back her own life, but keep Joey sufficiently in Rafaello's too? She didn't know. Only knew that *something*
had to be hammered out.

*Because I can't go back—I just can't. I can't, I can't,
I can't.*

Joey had run on indoors and she turned to shut the
front door behind her, shopping bags in her hands. As
she did so, she saw a taxi pulling up at the kerb. One of
the airport taxis.

Alaina froze.

Rafaello stepped out on to the pavement. Glanced towards
the narrow house. Saw Alaina at the doorway. Her face
had gone paper-white. He walked up to her, his gait steady,
his face expressionless, as the taxi moved off behind him.

He heard her say his name faintly, as though it were
costing her a lot. Costing her as much as it was costing
him to keep his face expressionless, to keep all emotion
out of his voice as he said her name in return.

'I would like to talk to you,' he said. He paused a moment. 'Is Joey here?'

She nodded, as though speech were beyond her. She

was still paper-white, but there was something in her face, her eyes…

She stepped aside, jerkily, and he walked in. Headed into the sitting room.

'Hello, Joey,' he said.

Joey whirled around. His face lit up like the sun. With a cry he hurled himself at Rafaello, and Rafaello swept him up. Joey's little arms wrapped themselves around his neck, his legs around his waist and Rafaello clutched him tightly, his heart pounding…hammering. Slowly, he lowered Joey to the floor.

Joey danced around him, exclaiming rapturously. 'Papà! Papà! Papà!'

Alaina was walking into the room. Joey went running up to her.

'Papà is here!' he told her, excitement vivid in his voice. Then he turned back to Rafaello. 'Are we going home?' he asked him.

Rafaello's eyes went to Alaina. For one impossible moment he held her stricken gaze. Then he lowered his to Joey.

'I need to talk to Mummy,' he said. 'Can you go up to your room and play on your own for a while?'

Joey looked fearful suddenly. 'You won't go, will you?'

Rafaello shook his head. 'No,' he said, 'I won't go.'

'OK, then,' Joey said. He rummaged in one of the shopping bags, pulled out a sizeable box. 'I've got a new train set!' he announced. 'I'm going to play with it!'

He thundered up the stairs.

Rafaello turned his attention to Alaina. She still looked white as a sheet.

A sense of déjà vu swept over him. She'd gone white as a sheet that evening he'd arrived here all those months ago, to tell her that now he knew of Joey's existence he would be a permanent fixture in his son's life. And that the most civilised way of achieving that was for them to marry and make a home for him in Italy.

It had seemed so simple. So straightforward. So obvious…

But now…

He saw her lower herself jerkily into the armchair opposite the small sofa, perching at the edge of the seat, just as she had all those months ago.

Then, she was simply a woman I had romanced five years earlier and then parted from.

But now…

The same words came again. Brief words…changing everything.

He drew a breath, let his eyes rest on her face.

'Why did you leave me, Alaina?' he asked.

Emotion was churning within her. Emotion that was impossible to control, to contain, to suppress or repress. It was filling her, consuming her, overwhelming her. Possessing her.

Her hands, clutching at each other, tightened their grip.

'I couldn't stay,' she said.

Her gaze was hooked on him.

He's here—real, solid, sitting a couple of metres away—and I can't bear it… I can't…

Something changed in his face. It had already been unreadable. But somehow it had become more so. Tension pulled across his shoulders, moved in every line of his body as he sat there.

So close to her.

So far away…

In the months she'd been with him—in the months since they had become lovers, come to know each other's bodies so intimately she could have recognised him in pitch-dark by touch alone—she had been able to reach for him, to be casually and easily in bodily contact with him. Leaning against him on the sofa...brushing his arm in passing...all those easy signs of companionship... Yet now he seemed a million miles distant from her.

And I've done it! I've made it this way.

Anguish clutched at her like a vice.

But I had to do it! I had to!

He was speaking again, and she made herself listen, block out the anguish that was crushing her like a vice, the same way her fingers were crushing each other in her lap.

'Can you explain to me why?'

His voice was neutral. As if he were addressing a client, drawing out from them just what their problem was.

She tried to find words. The words that would explain to him without explaining.

'I... I thought I could make it work...the arrangement we agreed on. I really thought I could. But—' the lump of concrete inside her throat made speaking difficult '—in the end I couldn't.'

'Can you say why?'

Again, he spoke in that neutral tone, drawing her out, gathering the information he needed to analyse the situation and then make his recommendations, as he would to a client, presenting them with their options.

But I don't have any options—only the one I've resorted to. The only one I can bear!

She tried to find a way of answering him that would not answer him. Not with the truth. The truth she could not speak.

Because what purpose would it serve? None. He would hear it, and note it, and then...

Then what? The truth of why she had left him, why she was divorcing him, was irrelevant. It would change nothing, and since it would change nothing there was no point telling it.

'It wasn't what I wanted,' she said. She sounded curt, but didn't mean to be.

His eyes rested on her. She couldn't read them. She never could. The only expression in his eyes she had ever been able to read was desire. That, and that alone, he had not veiled. Oh, she'd seen amusement in his eyes—wry, mostly, but warm, too, sometimes, when it was at something that Joey had done or said—but there had never been anything else. Approval, perhaps, when she'd appeared in an outfit he'd considered becoming on her, and said so. But his thoughts, his moods, his feelings—all those were never visible.

He was neither cold, like his father, nor hot. Just...cool. Cool and in control—not harshly so, but only ever composed and collected, calm and unruffled, unperturbed and unreadable. He was easy to be with. He was courteous and friendly, conversational and relaxed. But...

He holds the world at bay.

He held *her* at bay.

Oh, sexual desire had burned between them—dear God, how it had burned! But...

But nothing else.

She looked at him now. Accepted who he was.

I can't reach him.

The words fell into the space inside her head, sounding like a death knell.

He was speaking again, and she made herself listen—

though to what purpose she did not know. How would this conversation help at all? It couldn't.

'So what *did* you want?' he asked.

She heard the words, and in her head a thousand answers came. But none were any use—none at all. So there was no use saying them.

And yet...

She propelled herself to her feet. 'I wanted,' she said, 'what it is not in you to give.' She took a breath, and it was like a razor passing over her throat. 'I wanted to give what it is not in you to accept. And I'm sorry. I truly am. I tried... I tried not to want it. But it was too late.'

She looked down at him as he sat there on her little sofa, his long body showing tension in every line, though his face was still unreadable. She felt the concrete inside her swell until it possessed her whole body. He was so close to her—and yet he was a million miles away. In a place she could never reach.

She shut her eyes, defeated.

'I wanted you to love me,' she said.

CHAPTER FIFTEEN

RAFAELLO HEARD THE WORDS. They hung in the air. She had closed her eyes and he was glad of it. It let him go on looking at her.

He felt himself get to his feet. There seemed to be two of him suddenly, but he wasn't sure why.

I wanted you to love me.

The words had an echo of their own. An echo all around him. An echo reaching back...

And suddenly he wasn't there. Wasn't in this neat but unremarkable room, with its budget furniture and reproduction prints on the wall, its modest TV in the corner. He wasn't there at all.

He was in a hospital room. Well, not a hospital...a clinic. A discreet, very expensive clinic—for money could buy discretion, and that was important—tucked away in the Dolomites, where patients could benefit from the fresh mountain air. Patients who found life a little difficult from time to time. Patients with families who found *them* difficult...

He was looking down at the figure lying in the bed. Lying very still. In his head he heard the words the clinician had said to him, speaking very carefully—to a client...to a lawyer...

Explaining how there had been an adverse reaction to some medication…so very unfortunate…and impossible to foresee, given that the patient had—without the clinic's knowledge, of course—taken some medication of her own that she had secreted away…medication that had unfortunately not been compatible with what the clinic had prescribed.

'I am so very sorry,' the clinician had said.

Then he had left the room.

Leaving Rafaello alone.

With the body of his mother.

Who had wanted him to love her.

Alaina opened her eyes. She could not keep them shut for ever. She opened them, and swallowed, though there was still a razor in her throat. It was slicing through her vocal cords one by one, silencing her. But too late.

She had said the words to Rafaello she had sworn she never would because there would be no point saying them.

He was standing there, quite immobile. As immobile as she was. His face still had no expression in it. And yet…

There was something in his eyes. Something in those lidded, dark, occluded eyes that out of nowhere flashed with a light that was actually no light at all—but darkness. A visible darkness.

She felt her hand jerk forward—then pulled it back.

'I'm sorry,' she said. Her voice was low, all she could manage…a bare, strained husk. 'I should not have told you. There…there was no point in doing so. And it's… it's an irrelevance.'

She shut her eyes again for a moment, to give herself a moment's respite, then they flew open again.

'Rafaello, I'm sorry—I truly am. I tried so hard to stop myself. Just as—' She pressed her lips together, then spoke again. 'Just as I did five years ago. Then I succeeded. I had to. You drove away...you were not around any longer. I had to get on with my life. There was nothing else to be done. You weren't there.'

She felt her fingers tighten into fists, hanging by her sides.

'But when I was with you again...after we'd married... day after day...night after night...it started again. I tried to stop it—truly I did—but I failed. I *tried* to treat our marriage as you were treating it, for all the reasons you did. I truly thought, I could succeed! But when I saw Dante and Connie together, saw their marriage, saw what they are to each other...as we were not...could never be...I... I could not bear it—'

She gave up, defeat in her voice, a terrible weariness dragging at her. She rubbed a hand across her brow.

'I can't live with you, Rafaello, knowing that this time around I can't stop myself wanting what I wanted five years ago. Can't stop myself doing now what I managed at such cost not to do five years ago. I can't stop myself falling in love with you. Even knowing...' she felt her throat tighten in agony '...knowing nothing has changed since we first met. That falling in love with you now is as pointless...hopeless...as it would have been five years ago.'

She made herself take a breath, forced herself on.

'And...and because of that, I... I can't be with you on the terms you set out—the terms we live by in our marriage. I just can't do it. So please, *please* can we come to some other arrangement for Joey? Something that will give him an equal share of us both...that will be fair to all of us. Surely…oh, surely, with good will and effort we can achieve that. Can't we?'

Her voice was openly pleading. How could it be otherwise? So surely—oh, *please*—Rafaello would agree? Because he would no more want to live with a woman always wanting what he could not give than…

But he was speaking again, and his words were like stones. Dropping on her pleas. Crushing them to pieces.

'No,' he said. 'I don't think we can.'

She was staring at him. Her eyes—so very beautiful—distended and wide. Filled with anguish. She was going to speak, to say something, but he held up his hand.

'I don't think we can,' he said again.

Something was happening inside him. He could feel it. Those two people—that separation into two that he had felt as her words had echoed down the long years to him standing looking down at his mother's body, lying so defenceless in the bed at the clinic—were blurring.

'I don't think we can,' he said once more, letting his arm fall to his side. 'Because, you see, it would be quite impossible.'

She started. 'But we must… We *must*—for Joey's sake—find another way—'

'Yes,' he said. 'I think we must.'

He looked away for a moment. He knew there was a frown in his eyes. And something was pressing on him from the inside. He did not know the source of the pressure, but it was building with every moment. His eyes went back to Alaina. She was still standing stock still, her eyes huge, anguish in her face…

He felt that pressure still building within him. And then—in a moment, in an instant—it was gone—

That knife had plunged into his side again—between his ribs, into his lungs. It was an agonising pain. The same as he had felt by the empty pool at the empty villa. With Alaina and Joey gone.

His wife and his son—gone.

But now they're here. I'm with them again.

He felt the words rise up in him, moving through the pain possessing him.

They are here—and I will never—never!—lose them again.

Because to lose them would be an agony he could not endure.

I thought of her as the mother of my son—the woman I had to marry for that reason alone. Had to make my wife for that reason alone. A wife I did not choose and the son I felt responsible for, whose conception I would not have chosen either. But now...

Now everything was entirely and utterly different.

It's taken me till now to realise—to see. To feel what I am feeling now... To know.

To know that to lose either Joey or Alaina would be intolerable…unbearable…

He tried to speak, but his words were halting. He could not find them—though he had to. Words that must be framed in a language he had never spoken, never thought to speak.

But now he spoke.

Because not to speak would be an agony he could not endure.

'There is…there is a way,' he said, halting, hesitant,

feeling his way into a land that was stranger to him than a distant planet.

How can I find it? How can I make my way there? How can I?

He felt despair fill him, possess him utterly.

And then suddenly there were more words—but not his. It was the pleading, impassioned voice of the mother who had wanted him to love her, as she loved him, and loved the man she had married, who had no love to give to her or anyone. He heard her voice now as clearly as if she were alive still—had never met that sad, mistaken end all those years ago, bereft of all that she had so longed for.

'Oh, my darling—my darling one! You can find the way! You left it—but you can come back to it—find it again.'

Then his own words came. The words that would reach out, bring him to where the pain possessing him would stop, cease and be assuaged.

'You said...' The words were still hesitant, but growing in power as he spoke them. He could feel it...know it. 'You said you wanted me to love you.' His eyes held hers. 'What if I wanted the same? What if...?' he said—and now he felt his feet move, as if on an impulse that was not his own and yet at the same time more his own than any step he had ever taken. 'What if I *wanted* you to love me?' He took a breath. 'To love me back.'

She did not move. Only stood there. And for a moment—a terrible, agonising moment—he was back in that room in the clinic, his mother's lifeless body there in front of him. She had wanted him to love her, but it was too late...too late for him to do so...to tell her...

But now it was not too late—not too late to say what he must say...could not bear *not* to say.

'Alaina... I, too, thought that the marriage we had made

would work. That it would give our son a happy home...
that it would give us a life that would work on the terms
that we had come to. I thought that right up until you left
me. But when I went to the villa and you were not there,
and Joey was not there, and the place was empty, and
you were gone—then...then I knew the folly of it all. The
depths of my self-delusion.'

He took a step towards her. Reached for her hands,
lifted them in his. Hers were cold, so cold, and he closed
his own around them. She was staring up at him still, her
eyes so wide, so beautiful. He felt the pain slice into him
again, tightened his grip on her hands.

'All my life,' he said, 'I've kept my distance. It made
life...easy. When I parted with you five years ago it was
easy to do so. Then, when I found out about Joey's existence, it seemed...not easy, but less difficult to do what I
have done. To take you and him into my life, accommodate
you, fit you in, adapt to you. Honour my responsibilities to
my son...my obligation to you as his mother. That you just
happened to be even more beautiful now, as Joey's mother,
than you were five years earlier on a Caribbean island,
was, I admit, an attraction—a compensation, if you will,
for my having to change my life entirely because of Joey.'

He heard his voice twist, the wry note that came into it.

'And we were, you must admit, highly compatible in
that respect.'

A sensual note entered his voice—he could not help
it—and he lowered his eyes.

He saw colour run up her ashen cheeks and was glad
of it. His grip on her hands tightened yet more, lest she
seek to withdraw them. But she made no attempt. No
movement at all.

'I thought,' he said, 'that everything was as sorted as

it needed to be, and that between us there would be what we had together five years ago. As much as that, but… but nothing more.'

He took a breath, searching for words. Finding them. And now his voice changed yet again, became edged with the pain that was still hollowing him.

'But what I did not realise was that something else was happening. Joey—the son I was not sure how to be a father too…the kind of father he needed…the kind that I needed to be for him—was reaching into my heart.'

He stopped, taking another breath, holding her hands still fast in his.

'And so were you.'

For a timeless moment there was silence, and she was completely still. Her eyes stayed fixed on his, wide and distended, and in them…

He spoke again. Saying all he wanted to say…needed to say.

'I was becoming…dependent. On you,' he said. 'For staying alive. For breathing. For my very heart to keep beating…' His expression changed. 'I don't know love, Alaina. I've kept it far away. So I didn't recognise it. Never realised. Only when you left. Then your absence taught it to me in the desolation I felt in that empty house. Without you.'

He drew a breath, stepped closer to her, closing the distance between them. Closing it for ever. He could catch the faint perfume of her body, feel the warmth of her hands in his now.

'Do you think,' he asked, 'that now we might find a way forward? A way,' he said, 'to make our marriage work? A marriage in which we love each other—now and for ever.'

Tears were welling in her eyes. Like diamonds, but more beautiful. The most beautiful thing in the world. He heard her say his name, her voice catching, and it was all he needed.

His mouth kissed her tears away, then grazed her trembling lips as he drew her into his arms. A sense of relief so profound that it shook him possessed him. Her hands were slipping from his, wrapping him to her, and his arms came around her, holding her tight, so tight. Never, never to let her go.

And still he went on kissing her as he had never kissed her before. Because never before had she been the woman he loved.

As she was now.

Now and for ever...

A hand was tugging at his sleeve, a little voice piping up. The only voice he would ever attend to more than to that of the woman he now knew, with that sense of relief that shuddered through him, he loved for ever and for good.

He drew back, looking down at Joey.

'Come and see my new train set!' Joey said. 'Mummy too!'

Rafaello took his hand. His son's hand was so small in his, and so infinitely precious. The same love that swept through him for Alaina now swept through him for his son as well. Shaking him to the core with its intensity.

'Show me,' he said. 'And Mummy too.'

Joey needed no second invitation. He grabbed his mother's hand as well. She gave a laugh, carefree and joyous, and Joey tugged them both forward, then vaulted up the stairs.

Behind him, his parents followed.

Taking each other's hands again.

Never to let them go.

Alaina leant back against Rafaello on the banquette in the nearby popular family hostelry they'd repaired to for lunch, after admiring Joey's new train set.

Joey was busy with the crayons and colouring sheet the child-friendly restaurant had provided. Contentment radiated from him.

As for her...she felt a happiness so golden that she could not believe it.

La dolce vita—that is what I now truly, truly have! True, and wonderful, and blissful! The sweetness of life— loving Rafaello—him loving me back.

She turned now to Rafaello, his arm strong and safe around her shoulder, heart filled with love for him.

His eyes were shadowed. 'I was always torn,' he said, his voice low. She could hear the tension in it...the pain. 'Between my mother and my father. I tried to be a bridge between them, but it was impossible. They were so entirely different—extreme in their ways. You've met my father—cold and detached. My mother was the very opposite. Impassioned and emotional. She loved too much.'

'She loved,' said Alaina, her eyes full, never wanting to see that shadow in his eyes again, that grief, 'as my own mother loved. She loved a man who could not return that love.' Her face convulsed. 'Which is why I was so scared, Rafaello—*so* scared! Five years ago I pulled back in time—I had to. I told you. But this time...seeing you...living with you...being intimate with you... How could I stop myself? How could I?'

She seized his hand, pressing it close.

'Are you sure, Rafaello? Are you really, really sure?

Because I couldn't bear it—I just couldn't—if you woke up one morning and realised that you didn't…didn't love me after all…'

He meshed his fingers with hers, so tightly she winced.

'When…when my mother died, I… I changed,' he told her. 'Whether, as the official verdict told us, it was because of some lethal cross-reaction of her medication with a drug she'd self-administered, or whether…' his voice became more strained '…as I feared, she had knowingly taken those pills, her death made me…withdraw.'

He took a breath, filling his lungs. He lifted her hand to his lips, his fingers meshed with hers.

'I wanted my life to be as it became—without deep emotions. But now…'

He took her hand and placed it over his heart.

'Now I will love you till I die,' he said simply.

Tears filled her eyes, spilled over. 'Oh, my darling! My dearest, dearest one!' she said softly.

She kissed his mouth gently, with all the love in her heart. All the love she was now free to give, for he was now free to receive it from her, and offer her his in exchange.

For one long, endless moment they gazed into each other's eyes, hiding nothing. Giving everything.

Then Alaina felt her son's hand patting her arm.

'I've coloured in my picture,' he announced. A plaintive look crossed his face. 'Is my burger coming? My tummy is *very* hungry…'

'Mine too,' said Rafaello.

'And mine,' said Alaina.

'We're all in complete agreement,' Rafaello laughed.

On *everything*, thought Alaina.

And all the happiness of love drenched through her, along with the wonder of it all…the joy that would always be hers—theirs—now and for ever.

EPILOGUE

JOEY WAS SPLASHING in the pool. He was squealing with glee because Giorgio, standing at the edge, was directing the garden hose fully on to him, chortling as he did so.

Alaina laughed. 'I'm not sure who's the bigger kid,' she said.

She turned to look at Rafaello, lounging beside her on the swing seat they'd had installed. Joey adored it, but had had to be warned not to make it swing too widely or it would break.

'Speaking of kids,' she said, 'what do you think? Should we try for another? Or just be glad for Joey?' She gave a laugh. 'Connie's doing her best to persuade me to go for it!'

Rafaello laughed too. 'Dante is trying with me likewise. Especially now that Connie is expecting again.' He looked at Alaina. 'What do *you* think? You're the one who'll get pregnant.' A shadow crossed his face. 'You had to cope with your pregnancy with Joey all on your own… That weighs on me.'

Alaina shook her head. 'It was my call, and I made the one I felt was right at the time. But…'

She fell silent.

'We can't change the past,' Rafaello said quietly. 'We

can't change the fact that our own parents, in such similar ways, were unhappy with each other and that their unhappiness preyed on us. But we can change the future—we already have. And, however emotionally frozen our fathers were...*are*...we both know that our respective mothers would be happy for us.'

She reached for his hand. 'So very happy,' she said softly.

'And we must be happy for each other, too,' Rafaello said.

His voice was warm, and the warmth in it set a glow to Alaina's heart. The man she had thought so unreachable, so self-contained, so *apart*, was now as much a part of her as her beloved Joey was.

Her eyes went to her son...*their* son...and the glow intensified, joy welling up in her. How precious he was, her adored Joey...*their* adored Joey! How infinitely precious...

As precious as a brother or sister for him would be... A child who this time would be conceived with hope and hopefulness and above all with love. The love between her and Rafaello—flowing fully and freely and for ever...

Her gaze swept back to him, her husband and her beloved, the love of her life. No longer did she fear her mother's fate, for Rafaello returned her love, fulfilled it a thousand times, a million times, and his love was as deep as hers.

She lifted her mouth to kiss his cheek, smiling.

'I think,' she said, and her eyes were alight with longing, 'that Connie is a *wonderful* example to follow! So...' Her expression changed, and her lips moved from his cheek to graze softly and sensuously along his mouth 'How about it?'

His mouth caught hers, answering her kiss and her question.

'That, Signora Ranieri,' he said, his voice as low and as wickedly seductive as the glint in his dark eyes, 'is a very, *very* good observation. I heartily commend it.'

Alaina's hand reached to cup his cheek. 'Then let us not delay,' she said huskily. She kissed him enticingly. 'We could make a start this very night...'

Which was exactly what they did.

And for as many nights as it took.

Until one morning Alaina displayed the tiny tell-tale stick with the revealing blue lines on it and relayed the joyful tidings to Rafaello.

And then both of them reached for their phones and sent two short but highly communicative texts: Rafaello to Dante, and Alaina to Connie.

The delighted answers they received in return were exceeded only by the excitement evinced by Joey, bouncing up and down on the bed in glee as they told him that he just might be getting a baby brother or sister soon.

He eventually collapsed in a heap between them and they hugged him tightly—their wonderful, beloved son, who had brought them together not just in parenthood, not just in marriage, but in true and everlasting love.

They were a loving, devoted family—the way it should be. Always.

Above Joey's head, Rafaello leant across to kiss Alaina, his beloved wife, and Alaina kissed him back, her beloved husband. Perfect in their happiness.

* * * * *